Candace J. Boswell is a student at Tennessee State University. Born and raised in the Bronx, New York, Candace developed a passion for writing and storytelling at a young age. She is an avid reader who enjoys various genres, including fantasy, historical fiction, and romance. Her love of storytelling matured with her love of the performing arts, notably competitive dance, and theatre. When the 2020 global pandemic hit during her junior year of high school, Candace used her free time to dream up stories. The pandemic gave her the excuse and leisure time to explore and write them down.

To Young Writers

Don't be afraid to tell your story. You are never too young to start. Be tenacious and bold and remain true to yourself. Your journey is written in the stars.

Candace J. Boswell

# 13 LIVES

AUSTIN MACAULEY PUBLISHERS™

LONDON * CAMBRIDGE * NEW YORK * SHARJAH

**Ordering Information**
Quantity sales: Special discounts are available on quantity purchases by corporations, associations, and others. For details, contact the publisher at the address below.

**Publisher's Cataloging-in-Publication data**
Boswell, Candace J.
13 Lives

ISBN 9781685624156 (Paperback)
ISBN 9781685624163 (ePub e-book)

Library of Congress Control Number: 2023905044

www.austinmacauley.com/us

First Published 2023
Austin Macauley Publishers LLC
40 Wall Street, 33rd Floor, Suite 3302
New York, NY 10005
USA

mail-usa@austinmacauley.com
+1 (646) 5125767

My story is largely about love, loving yourself, your family, your friends and accepting the love of a partner. So, in true thematic fashion, I dedicate my story to all the people I love, who helped make this possible.

To my parents, thank you for supporting me through my journey and raising a bookworm and nurturing the creativity surging within me. Dad, you pushed me to be my best and offered advice every step of the way. The look of pride on your face gave me the motivation to open my computer and write, every single day. Mom, my best friend, you were my rock through this entire experience. You are this story's heart and soul.

To BJ, thank for all the late nights and long conversations, listening to me talk about these characters and my plans for their story.
To Kristen and Jason, thanks for all the love.

To my fourth grade teacher, Mrs. Phillip, you fostered a love for reading and writing in me. Thank you for guiding me to my passion. I haven't seen you in years, but I hope you see this one day and you remember the shy, quiet little girl whose world you expanded, and I hope you are proud.

And lastly, to the reader, as you embark on this literary journey, remember your worth. Love and respect yourself and your individual journey with every fiber of your being. Protect your soul, for it has endured the hardships of life. Open your heart to the unconditional love you deserve. My characters experienced a traumatic event and throughout the story, a major theme is self – discovery and learning to love who are. And by accepting yourself, you become capable of letting others in. Thank you for reading my book. I hope this story and the characters bring you the same joy they have brought me.

I love you all.
Sincerely,
Me

# Table of Contents

# 1. Where the Beauty Lies

I never really thought about death, although it is always around. It hangs over all of us, the sword of Damocles, a shadow chasing you until the darkness snuffs out the light. I never registered how isolating it is, how final it feels. And I can't escape its pull on me.

My story starts in a place with bountiful love and quickly submerges into the vast waters of hate and cruelty. My name is Margaret Baker. I am nineteen years old, and March 12, 1693, was the worst day of my entire existence.

I remember the day so clearly. The way the sun torched intolerably in the sky, the smell of the spring flowers in bloom, the cries of the people I hold dear. It was the day my childhood ended; my innocence violently stripped. The pure white drape of security and the rose-colored glasses through which I saw the world was taken from me, forcing me to grow up and learn to combat the hatred and evil that infiltrates the world around me.

I woke up that morning wide-eyed and bushy-tailed. The little hovel I called home was filled with the smell of mother's porridge. I rose from my bed, eager to begin the day.

My mother, Jean Baker, had agreed to let me participate in a coven meeting. I had attended them since I was old enough to walk but was always instructed to observe. My eyes filled with wonder watching my parents, the regents in our neighborhood, lead our coven. I practiced spells at home but never during official coven assignments. Those spells were entrusted to the elders and people who proved their allegiance through studying the craft and completing the most intricate and complex spells. I had been waiting for that moment my entire life and when that day arrived, an overwhelming amount of excitement rushed through me. I sprinted to the washroom to get ready for my day. I put on my favorite dress, a pale pink tea gown with peasant sleeves and a high neckline. I styled my curls in a half-up half-down style with a flower crown. This momentous day required a festive outfit to match the joyous occasion that lies in store. I made my way to the kitchen with a quickness. My mother was singing a sweet melody and illuminating our home with her cheer. Her bountiful compassion and sunny disposition were unmatched. Her love engulfed me, leaving me with a perpetual feeling of comfort and happiness. She truly felt comfort in giving aid to others, her most admirable quality. It made her a wonderful regent and a beautiful person. I danced over to my mother and kissed her cheek as she stirred the porridge.

My mother beamed. "Your beauty is exquisite, my dear."

My father, Edmund Baker, sat at our table reading the family grimoire as he did every morning. He looked up at me and a smile stretched on his concentrated form.

"You certainly are a fair maiden, Maggie."

Father spent his days working as a baker and engrossed his spare time in studying grimoires and creating enchantments. He tirelessly served our community, giving his family a comfortable life. His sacrifice and love were overwhelming.

He met my mother's eyes, "Your beauty matches that of your mother."

I began to recall the details of their first meeting. My mother, a young maiden, paid a visit to my grandfather's bakery before my father inherited it. She wore a mint green corset and petticoat. Her hair was styled in a pinned curls updo under a matching green bonnet. My mother was the epitome of beauty and came from a particularly wealthy family. My mother did not care for finance or status but instead the depths of her love. She was willing to leave behind her lavish life to be with the man who made her world turn. My father, then a young man, wore a white collared shirt under an apron soiled with flour and placed an assortment of danishes on the display counter. My mother asked for a cheese danish. They chattered about how peculiar that choice is. My mother continued to visit the bakery for a year. Father walked with my mother every afternoon to a nearby lake after the bakery closed at night. They spoke about their biggest dream and desires. They bonded over their love of witchcraft and affinity for a family. After asking for her father's permission, he proposed to her at the lake during a cheese danish picnic, and brunch. Their love story is the best I have ever heard. In my eyes, their love beat Romeo and Juliet. Their love encompassed me, and I put it on a pedestal. I hoped to find a love that consumes me the way theirs did.

My older sister, Joan entered the room and pulled me out of my memory. She embraced me from behind and wished me luck on my big day.

"You look marvelous, little sister," said Joan.

I blushed at her affections. Joan swiftly kissed both of our parents on the cheeks and took a seat to the right of Father, who is seated at the head of the table. I sat down next to her.

"Are you meeting with Charles, today," I said inquisitively. My twenty-two-year-old sister was courting a warlock from our coven. She spent every waking day with him. Their love was intoxicating. They have been courting for about a year. I wondered when I would be notified of a proposal. I was a hopeless romantic and yearned to be a bridesmaid.

"Yes, we are going down to the town square at noon."

I furrowed my brow at this, and Joan let out a long-frustrated sigh.

"Don't fret, Maggie. I will return before, lunch, just in time for your meeting." Joan adjusted my flower crown and then took my hand in hers. Joan gave it a gentle squeeze before meeting my gaze and shooting me a reassuring smile.

"Thanks, Jo." I beamed. I shot her a mischievous smile.

I pointed at a vase of white roses in the center of the table. We concentrated on it for several seconds before joining hands.

We chanted, "Resurgemus."

The vase began to hover over the table. A smile stretched across Father's face. He looked at us with immense pride for successfully completing the spell. He applauded our efforts before returning to his reading. After keeping the vase in the air for a minute, Joan gave me a nudge. I interpreted this as her saying to conclude the spell.

I chanted, "Retornen."

Mother gestured to Joan, and she rose from the table to assist her in serving the porridge. I love how close my family is. I took their support and warmth for granted. I did not realize how breathtaking that was until I lost it. My mother took a seat to the left of my father and my sister returned to her seat next to me after they served the meal. We blessed the food before consuming it. We discussed our plans for the day as we ate. It was a quiet morning full of anticipation and excitement. It was a moderately warm spring day and the neighborhood stood still. This was the quiet before the treacherous storm.

# 2. Elixir of Life

We had heard whispers of the Witch Trials in Salem, but Father thought it was a hoax to scare witches into hiding. He was a proud man and was not going to suppress a part of himself on the premise of hear-say. I would love to have someone to blame, but the truth is none of us genuinely believed in it. We were naïve in our safe bubble in our little city in Massachusetts. I remember whispering to Joan about the fabric I wanted to purchase from the nearest shop. I was saving up my money to make a dress for Mother for her birthday, and I required her assistance. Our conversation was interrupted by nearby screams.

Father met our eyes and place a long figure over his lip. He motioned at us to be silent. He swiftly approached the window and smoothed back the curtains to see the neighborhood in ruins. Men with large firearms were kicking open doors of select houses, forcefully removing residents, and setting their houses aflame. His skin paled. I watched my father, a very steady man, begin to shake nervously as he closed the curtains. My mother gasped at his response. He turned to meet our gaze.

He took a deep breath and commanded, "Joan run to the lair now and get the Elixir!"

Joan cried, "Yes, Father." She moved with a quickness. I stared at Father, confused by his demeanor and haste.

I protested, "What is happening? Why do we need the elixir?"

He ignored my questions and ran to the fireplace to start a fire. Mother moved to the bookshelf in the far corner of the room. She began to gather all the grimoires.

I cried, "Please tell me what is happening? You're scaring me!"

Mother shot me a sympathetic glance.

She whispered, "Darling they are looking for witches. The Salem Trials are real. We need to rid ourselves of any evidence that can incriminate us."

Mother met Father at the fireplace and threw the books in.

My family's greatest spells were dying with my childhood and hope for humanity. Overcome with emotion for the loss of this family heirloom, I began to sob. Mother ran over to me. She removed the silver pendant from around her neck and paced it on me. She smoothed a strand of hair out of my face and kissed my forehead. She caressed my cheek as my eyes filled with tears.

She soothed me, "Promise me that this will not change you. This occurrence cannot hinder the light in your heart. The world thinks were monsters, but I want you to study that pendant and remember the truth whenever your mind agrees with their falsities. Love yourself despite the circumstance the world creates to make you falter toward the opposite, my dear."

My heart rate eased as I turned the pendant over between my finger and replayed her words. She pulled away from me and returned to Father. He was prodding the burning books with a metal rod.

Joan raced back into the room with a glass bottle with pale pink liquid. She handed the elixir to Mother. I recognize the bottle and the memory of learning about the Elixir of Life in a coven meeting came rushing back to me. Legend says that the potion was made from the ashes of the Tree of Life. It grants thirteen lives to the people who consume a drop of it.

Father whispered, "Did you seal off the lair with the protection spell?" Joan nodded.

Mother said, "Let Margaret take it first." She scurried to me. She placed the glass bottle in my hand. I hesitated. While this did not necessarily grant me immortality, thirteen lifetimes were a lot to endure. Mother placed her hand on my shoulder, steadying me. I took a deep breath before taking a sip. I did not feel any different. I handed it to my mother as our door came crashing down.

Six men dressed in black with firearms entered our home. Father walked toward them with his hands in the air.

"What is the meaning of this intrusion," he questioned.

A tall muscular man met Father's gaze and yelled, "We are cleansing this land of vermin, devil spawn!"

Mother hid the vial behind her back. The same man noticed Mother's stance and approached her. He grabbed her by the waist and pulled her body close to his. Father cringed. His face turned red with fury.

The man whispered in her ear, "Turn around slowly for me love." She did as he commanded. The mysterious liquid in the glass bottle confirmed their theory about us. The man chuckled. I stared at this exchange astonished. I did not even know his name. He was destroying my life, my happy existence, and he remained nameless. He snatched the vile from her hands and threw it into the fireplace, I watched the hope dim from my mother's eyes as the flames engulfed it.

"No," I shouted and leaped toward it in an ineffectual attempt to retrieve it.

The man commanded, "Men, dispose of the freaks."

They restrained us with copper handcuffs. This element stung our skin while interfering with our magic. They marched us out of our home. We were instructed to stand still as they burned our home to the ground. I watched tears fall from my parent's eyes as the happy home they built turned to ash. The men began to take us in different directions, splitting us up.

My sister wailed, "Please. Do not do this! Let me go!" She struggled in their arms.

My father sharply turned toward her and yelled, "Be calm! Do not let them take away your dignity! We love you!"

The same man who gave the order to exterminate us approached me. I squirmed at the sight of him. He cupped my face, and I rejected his advances, turning my head away. He placed a potato sack over my head and then quickly walked with us to an undisclosed location. My heart raced as I wondered where they were taking me and what would happen to my family. I was the only one who took the elixir, so they were not safe. If these men were cruel enough to take their lives, they would not come back. I would have to carry on without them. This thought caused my stomach to churn, and I felt nauseated. I stumbled over my feet and landed on my knees.

A man's voice rang in my ears, "On your feet!"

I did as the voices said fearing the repercussions of disobedience. We walked for what felt like an eternity. Eventually, I was ordered to standstill. I felt the copper loosen and my arms were placed behind something massive and wooden. It was a stake. I felt a sense of relief as the pain stopped. My magic was still weak from the lengthy exposure to the cooper so defending myself was not an option. Someone placed the cuffs back on my hands. I whimpered as the cooper seared my skin. My whimpering made the men pull tighter. I was distracted from my own experience by the sounds of intense screams and a peculiar scent. A man removed the sack from over my head. The air was full of smoke. The sun blazed in the cloudy sky. I took shallow breaths due to the harsh conditions. I soon realized that the scent was burning flesh. My family was going to burn to death. I looked around wildly. Panic rushed through me. I screamed intensely. I could feel the capillaries bursting in my face, and I cried out for the lives of the people I loved.

I begged, "Please. My sister is only twenty-two, she has not lived yet. I have not had enough time with my family. I am a teenager, a child. Do not take my family from me. We can be good! We will be good! Just, do not take them away from me!"

I saw a pang of guilt surface on the face of one of the men. I locked eyes with him, hoping he would see my humanity. He turned away. This gave me a glimmer of hope, there was a small piece of humility within him.

I sobbed, "Do you have a daughter or even a wife?...A person you would protect until your last dying breath. My family is my everything. My sister is in love. I think she may get married soon if you give her more time. Please let us live in peace. We will not harm you. There is no need to fear us. We use our gifts to help people. We heal wounds and restore lands…"

"Stop talking freak," he interrupted. I could see the conflict in his eyes.

I begged, "Please stop this!"

He shouted, "I said stop!"

I took three blows to the face. Astonished by this act of violence, I stayed quiet. I feared his fist dancing across my face again. I thought of my mother's earlier words, "Love yourself despite the circumstance the world creates to make you lean toward the opposite, my dear." I held on to her love as I anxiously awaited my temporary death and my family's permanent one. I vowed to myself that I would not become the monster that they wanted me to be.

I looked across from me and noted a man walking my mother to a stake across from me. They took the bag from over her head. She stood tall as they cuffed her to the stake. I was in awe of her grace in even the most trying circumstances. A man walked toward her with a torch. Her eyes closed. I assumed she was praying. I wondered what her last thoughts were at that moment. Was she cursing the men? Or maybe she was begging that her family was safe. I will never know the answer to this question.

She looked up at me and yelled, "I love you!"

I screamed, "No! No! Please do not touch her! Do not take her from me!" The man threw the torch at her feet. I watched as she screamed in agony as her flesh melted away and turned to ash in front of my eyes.

I sobbed. The same man who was a permanent fixture in my thoughts, the one who sentenced my loved ones to a permanent slumber approached me. He caressed my cheek.

"Do not fret, little witch. You will join her soon."

Another man handed him a torch and he threw it at my feet. He ran several feet away from me. The fire spread throughout my body as I screamed in agony. His face was the last thing I ever saw in this life. I remember my world going black. I felt cold and isolated from the world.

I woke up several hours later. The sky was black. I was naked, only wearing my mother's pendant. I wildly looked around for something to cover me up. I spotted an abandoned cloak near a sake a few feet away from me. I quickly put it on and walked over to where my mother died, I cried over her remains. My anger and grief began to consume me. I cursed the memories of the men who did this to her. I remembered their faces and their lack of remorse. I hoped they suffered for their actions. I dug a hole by a nearby tree and placed her ashes inside. I searched frantically for a sharp object. I found a pocketknife in the cloak. I carved the words "RIP Jean" on the tree bark. I cried, acknowledging that I could not lay my sister and father to rest, unaware of their location. I sobbed at this realization. After an hour of crying over my mother's resting place, an elderly woman approached me.

"Poor child," she soothed. She placed a hand on my shoulder. I flinched, readying my body to defend myself.

She said, "I am like you. I am a member of your coven. I saw your pendant and realized that you must be Mary and Edmund's daughter." As her face came into focus, I realized that I did indeed recognize her. She pulled me up, and I sobbed in her arms. She pulled me into her chest and caressed my hair. A chestnut brown strand fell in front of my line of sight. My hair used to be jet black. The change of hair color alarmed me. Sensing my anxiety, the elderly woman, Mrs. Abbott, walked with me.

"There is a sanctuary that a few of us fled to when the rumors of the trial first surfaced. We will be safe there. My son and I were going there is seek refuge, but they rounded him up before we could embark on the journey." She sighed. Her face was pinched as she relived the memory.

"The sanctuary is a few miles from here. It is necessary to take the back roads and travel on foot to avoid being discovered." I nodded, feeling choked. I was unable to speak, drowning in a tsunami of grief. I remained silent throughout the entire journey and Mrs. Abbott, empathizing with my anguish, did not force a conversation.

We arrived at the sanctuary several hours later. I was offered food by a slender young adult witch with red hair and fair skin. I denied it, feeling nauseated from the loss of my family.

"Do you have a restroom?" I asked.

"Yes, down the hall, first door on the right…Oh, my name is Eliza by the way."

"Maggie," I responded. I found my way to the bathroom and immediately viewed my reflection in the mirror. My skin was a little paler than usual. My face was more rounded, and my cheekbones were more pronounced. I recalled my parents talking about how you reemerge at the same age every time you die after taking the elixir. My chest was more pronounced, and my hips were wider. My hair had looser curls. I marveled at my new body. I scrambled to grasp my opinions. Was this an upgrade? I was saddened that I no longer looked like my mother, the most beautiful woman I had ever seen. She was my definition of beauty. Today was supposed to be a celebratory day. I wept quietly, attempting not to make too much noise. I had a new life ahead of me, without the people who previously anchored me to the Earth. The ones who made every day worthwhile. I thought of the people who destroyed my life. And I concluded, there is no hell…because the devil walks among us.

# 3. Brave New World

Today is May 13, 2015. It has been three hundred and twenty-two years since my family's untimely demise. I have died of natural causes five times since that day. I am down to seven lives now. My second death was caused by a fever. The third through fifth were caused by old age. I now have chocolate skin with waist-length dark brown tightly curled hair, pronounced cheek bones, a slender build, and I stand five feet tall. I have kept to myself throughout the years, resisting long-term relationships. I now live in a small apartment in New York City and my work keeps me busy. I am a twenty-five-year-old kindergarten teacher at St. Ann's Elementary School. My students are my entire world.

I still wear my mother's silver pendant. I feel like I am close to my family and my old content life when I wear it. I have not practiced magic since my sister and I levitated the vase of white roses. I miss having the energy coursing through my veins, the satisfaction from successfully mastering a new spell. I wish I could say that I could not find a need for the use of magic, but I stopped because of fear. I am furious that I let those men take such a huge part of me.

With Mother's reassuring words still ringing in my head, I did not let the world convert me into an inhumane monster. I did not attempt to invoke violence on the mortals who stole my innocence, although I wanted to. I wanted the world to suffer the way I did. I wanted to scream at the top of my lungs, revealing my tragedy to the world.

My people have been forgotten. Our plight and massacre have been ignored for centuries and it revolts me. We are a riveting plot device in books and movies, interpreting our lives as fantasy. Stories of the Witch Trials are a campfire ghost story. How could these people be so blind? They fail to see what is right in front of them. The ache in my heart, the chip on my shoulder, and the protective walls I place around me are concrete.

I want to disclose my past, but I know how it will sound to the mortals. I will be viewed as a danger to myself and society, a delusional little girl attempting to rewrite a carefully buried history. I would be shipped off to an insane asylum, being heavily medicated and conditioned to deny my truth. So, I remain quiet and alone.

I tidied up my classroom, placing crayons and papers in their respective containers. My students left for the weekend. I swept the floor and erased my writing on the chalkboard. I grabbed my backpack and tan spring jacket, before exiting the building and began walking home. I lived a few blocks away from the school.

I briskly walked into my apartment building and hurried past the lobby, avoiding my doorman, Alex Brown. He attempted to make small talk with me nearly every day. He has also made a substandard attempt in courting me. His kindness was sweet but not very enticing to me. I am a freak, a loner, a nobody just trying to get by. Alex did not look my way today. Did he finally get the hint? His rejection unexpectedly saddened me. I had grown accustomed to his gestures and sad attempts at forming a meaningful relationship with me. Had my true, grotesque form somehow come bubbling to the surface?

I pushed these thoughts aside as I hurried to the staircase and climbed them to the third floor. I walked to apartment door 313 and sighed contentedly. I pulled my keys out of the side pocket of my bag once I reached the door. I entered my humble home, a small one-bedroom apartment. It consists of three rooms, a small bathroom, a bedroom, and a kitchen/living room area. The apartment was dull. I did not exert much effort in decorating. The walls are white and bare, complemented by the drab gray carpet. I ran in and threw my bag on the floor. A window stands across from the front door. My apartment has an impeccable view of 42$^{nd}$ street. The hustle and bustle and cheer of the city were intoxicating. The blinds always remained closed, isolating me from the outside. I hung my coat up in the closet adjacent to the door and then sat on my black sofa with gray pillows. I have a coffee table with a few cinnamon-scented candles in the center and a 40-inch flat-screen. I think that I subconsciously took up residence in New York to fill a void in my life. The streets are always congested with tourists, performers, and vendors. I expected to feel comforted by them, but I have never felt more secluded. I turned on the television and began to watch One Tree Hill reruns. My mind flittered with the dramatic lives of Ravens.

I carried on like this for two hours. I looked at my phone and saw the time. It was five o'clock in the afternoon. I walked over to my fridge to prepare dinner. To my surprise, my fridge was basically empty. Its contents included a carton of oat milk and bread. I inhaled deeply, annoyed by this inconvenience. I closed the fridge and returned to my slumped position on the couch. I decided to order food. I pulled out my phone to view my local options. I attempted to get Thai food delivered from a local restaurant. I called the store eager to get my food. My annoyance intensified when they claimed not to offer a delivery service.

I angrily grabbed my coat and swiftly put it on. I picked up my black Jan. sports bag that I had thrown on the floor upon my arrival and placed it on my back. I raced down an endless flight of stairs and out of the building. I pulled my phone out of my back pocket and put on headphones. I walked looking down at my phone and readying my playlist. Preoccupied with my phone, I bumped into a tall man with dark skin, and short jet-black curls. He wore a black tracksuit and carried a satchel.

"I am so sorry," I apologized. I removed the headphones from my ears.

He chuckled. "That's alright. Is your cell phone, OK? You stared at it so intensely."

I laughed awkwardly. "Umm…It's OK. I was trying to find a good song to listen to."

He smiled. "I can help with that. I am a music afficionado." He pulled out his phone. He scrolled through his playlist and looked up and studied me multiple times.

"I got the perfect song for you, 'When He Sees Me from Waitress the Musical.'"

I smiled. "…A musical?"

"What's wrong with a little musical theatre?" he protested.

"I have never seen a show. It's not really my thing," I said. I began to walk away.

"Come on, there is a musical out there for everyone," he said. I turned back around and rolled my eyes.

"Hmm…I have a proposition for you. Come with me to a show and then decide whether it is for you."

"I don't even know your name," I responded.

"Nathan, but my friends call me Nate." He extended his hand toward me. I grasped his hand and shook it lightly.

"I'm Margaret."

He grinned at me. I felt a sincere smile stretch across my face. Nate had this sparkle in his eyes, a genuine kindness about him. I wondered about the nature of his flirtatious advances. What was so special about me? In a city populated by 8.4 million people, he chooses to make advances toward me. Why was I entertaining it? Were the centuries of loneliness taking a toll on me? Was I so desperate for human contact?

He interrupted my train of thought.

"OK, Margaret. Let's go."

"Now!" I replied stunned.

"Yeah, I have a performance in about an hour. See the world through my eyes for a little while." I blushed, blood rushing to my cheeks as a physical manifestation of his kindness.

I needed this. For a moment, I remember the girl I used to be. Someone who believed in love and the fairness of humanity. I realized that I could no longer swallow my grief and carry my despair. I wanted to be genuinely happy for a moment. I wanted my sparkle, my hope back. I needed to claim it for myself, rise from the ashes. I took a chance on Nate. He could have been anyone at the moment. I felt something special in him. I couldn't quite put my finger on it, but I trusted him with my life. I had only known him for a few minutes, but I somehow knew he wouldn't hurt me. He was a perfect stranger, but he made me feel seen and safe. His gesture made me feel more comfortable in my body. I no longer felt the need to shrink, receding to a corner of the world. I thought that he could be the friend, I didn't know I needed. He took my hand in his and walked with me.

An unidentifiable feeling swelled inside of me. I thought that we were meant to be in each other's lives. Chance brought us together. I had never felt this way about anyone in my entire existence. Could he feel it too? I pushed these thoughts away, repulsed by the quickness at which I dreamt them up. I have too much baggage. He sees an unaccompanied young woman, but the truth is, I am older than I look. I have been through more pain and heartbreak than he could ever imagine. I continued to walk with him, but I vowed not to get attached. This life is temporary for him. I have seven more to endure.

Exposing my bleeding battered heart will only open the door to more heartbreak.

# 4. Welcome to Broadway

We approached the theatre through the stage door. His picture was plastered on the wall to the left of the door. I stared back at him in amazement.

"Wow, good-looking pic. You look important up there."

"Oh, that old thing. I forgot it was there." He smirked. He walked around to the front of the theatre. He took me back to his dressing room.

He knocked on the door.

"Everyone decent?"

"Yep," a man's voice shouted.

"Ok, first stop on the tour, the dressing room."

He opened the door and motioned for me to follow him.

"This is where we get dressed, hang out, warm up and fluff our hair before the show. Meet the guys. Guys, this is Margaret. They are great people and pretty decent singers." They all laughed.

I waved, sheepishly.

A bald man dressed in sweats approached me.

"Hey, good looking. What are you doing hanging out with Nate?" I chuckled awkwardly.

"OK, let's go before they scare you away," Nathan said. We made our way back into the hallway. We walked a few doors down. He opened the door, and I peered my head in.

"This is the costume room. It contains all the wardrobes for the show. We shouldn't touch anything."

I marveled at the outfits. I was particularly fond of a pink ball gown that hung on a clothing rack at the far corner of the room. We walked to the end of the hall, and he opened the door. The room did not have any staff in there yet, but the shelves were full of wigs.

"Last stop on the tour is the audience," Nate spoke. He walked with me to a ticket teller, at the front of the theatre.

"Hey, Brody. My main man…Uh, I was wondering if you could hook me up with a ticket for tonight."

"Dude, the show starts in 50 minutes," Brody whined.

"Come on. I know tonight's show isn't sold out."

"We have seats in the back row."

Nate side-eyed him.

"Dude, this is her first show ever. Let's give her a show she'll never forget. Do it for the art, man?"

Brody rolled his eyes. "How is seat 113 E," he asked. Nathan shot him a weary look and Brody returned his expression with a look of annoyance.

"We'll take it!" Nate announced. He handed me the ticket.

He twisted back to Brody, "Thanks, man."

He faced me again.

"I have to go get ready. See you after." He walked back toward the dressing rooms. Brody pointed me in the direction of a line of people waiting to be seated. I stood in line contemplating my choice to come with him. I stood online for a few minutes before being directed to my seat by an usher. Eventually, the room got dark, and the curtains opened. Revealing a magical set. I inhaled deeply, unaware of the magnificent journey that awaited me.

2 hours and 45 minutes later

The show was extraordinary, like nothing I had ever seen before. The grace and movement quality left me in awe. The story brought me to tears. I chuckled at the irony of a witch falling in love with a human and ignoring the reasons they must distance themselves from each other due to the strength of their affection toward one another. They fake their own deaths to be together. They got a happy ending. I knew the story was fiction, however, it gave me hope. I wanted that. I wanted to love someone so intensely that I would be willing to defy every odd to be near them. I want to feel love again. I am ready to reopen my heart and share a meaningful intentional experience.

I applauded wildly as he took his final bow. As people began to leave the theatre, I sat there pondering what I had just witnessed. I eagerly waited for Nathan to return to me. I sat alone with my thoughts for a few minutes. Nathan danced over to me. He was wearing his tracksuit and satchel again.

"You were amazing! That was the most breathtaking thing I have ever seen! Do you do that every night?" I exclaimed in one breath.

"Slow down," he playfully teased.

"I am sorry. It's all just so fascinating," I blushed.

He took my hand. "You trust me," he asked. I nodded. He hoisted me onto the stage and then climbed up.

"Dance with me," he said.

"I don't dance." I bit my lip and studied his expression.

"Sure, you do. Everyone dances. There is no right or wrong. Just move organically."

"OK, but you can't make fun of me." I sighed.

He chuckled. "No promises." I rolled my eyes and scuffed at him.

"Come on. Turn off your mind for two minutes and dance with me. I won't judge you." He pulled his phone out of his back pocket. He played a song I didn't recognize.

I shook my head in disagreement. "This is ridiculous. I am not a dancer, and I don't know you."

I walked upstage. I turned to face him hesitant to leave, and he shot me a reassuring smile. I approached him slowly. I took a deep breath and took his hand. He took my other hand in his and placed both on his shoulders.

"Just, let go and follow the music. Allow it to overtake you."

He grabbed my waist and pulled me toward him. I stared into his dark brown eyes and wondered what he was thinking as we swayed. The music slowed and his movement matched the change. I followed his lead. I listened to the words of the song and realize this must be the song he recommended earlier. I started to listen to the lyrics. It is about a girl who is afraid to fall in love, someone who hides from the unknown, and a woman afraid of showing vulnerability. She tries to convince herself that she is fine alone, escaping heartbreak, but ultimately evading love. The music sped up again, and we match the tempo. We waltz across the stage.

A smile formed on my face. I was having fun and for the first time in centuries, I did not feel guilty. We stared into each other's eyes. He twirled me around a few times and then dipped me and as the song reached its final few notes, he pulled me close. We stared into each other's eyes. He crouched down to meet me. I felt his warm breath against my face and our lips touched. Fireworks erupted in my head. I was having my first kiss and it was everything

I dreamt it would be. We continued for a short while. I pulled away and he tucked a strand of hair behind my ear.

"You're incredible," I blurted out.

"Thanks! You're not too bad yourself." We laughed simultaneously.

"Hey, can I show you something?" I nodded, not wanting this night to end. We walked together down a long hallway past empty dressing rooms.

"Brace yourself." He chuckled.

He opened the stage door, revealing a crowd of fans that screamed in response to his appearance. I gasped astonished by this development. He held my hand and walked me toward the crowd. I watched him sign autographs and take selfies with adoring fans. He had this air about him, a charisma, that made him so likable. He was kind to everyone that approached him. He engaged in lengthy conversations, making sure everyone was taken care of. I found it endearing that he cared so much about these people. He engaged with the fans for about forty-five minutes. He looked over at me several times, inspecting my demeanor. He was surrounded by so many but still saw the importance of my well-being. His voice broke me out of my contemplation.

"Thank you all so much. I need to go home for the night. I appreciate every one of you," he announced. He walked back over to me. He placed his arm around me and walked me inside.

"I have one more surprise."

"What other surprises could you have up your sleeve?" I giggled.

"I don't know…You hungry?"

"A little." That was an understatement. I was hungry three hours ago, now I am famished.

"Great, come with me."

We exited the theatre. We walked to the edge of the sidewalk. He waved his arms frantically and yelled, "Taxi! Taxi!"

A yellow taxi drove over to us almost immediately. I smiled at him excited to continue our journey. He opened the back door and said, "After you." I climbed inside and he followed me.

"Where are we going," asked the driver.

"Tom's Pizza," Nate said. The driver put the location into his GPS and drove away.

"We should get there in like five minutes," said the driver.

"Thanks, man," Nate responded. The driver shook his head.

28

Nathan turned to me.

"Have you been to Tom's before?"

"No, I usually go to Mario's Pizza. It is closer to my apartment."

"You have to try this pizza. It is the best in New York." I smiled at him. My phone buzzed in my pocket. I received an email from a parent. A parent had questions about a homework assignment. Typically, I would respond right away. But I was enjoying myself. I owed it to myself to stay in the moment. I checked the time. It was 9:30 pm. I don't usually stay out this late. I would be home creating lesson plans or watching a movie.

"Something wrong," Nate questioned.

"Nothing. Just work," I reassured.

"So, you know what I do for a living. Tell me what you do."

"I am a teacher."

"What grade?"

"Kindergarten."

"Oh, so you shape young minds...inspirational."

"I wouldn't say all that. I love what I do though. My kids mean the world to me."

"I get what you mean. I love being on stage, telling stories through the arts. The rest of the world disappears and even my own identity. I become my character as soon as the spotlight hits me. Hearing the cheers and feeding off the audience's energy and knowing that I connected with someone on that level melts my heart."

I met his gaze and grinned. "How could this man be so perfect?"

The driver pulled over.

"You owe me ten bucks." I reached in my backpack.

Nathan tapped my shoulder and said, "Allow me." He reached into his bag and pulled out a black leather wallet. He gave the man a twenty-dollar bill and said, "Thanks for the ride."

He exited the car and waited for me to exit after him. We walked into the store and took a seat at the table closest to the door.

A woman approached us and said, "The shop closes in half an hour."

"We'll be done by then," Nathan claimed.

"OK, then. What will you two be having?" She pulled a pen and notepad from her apron.

Nate gestured to me. "Ladies first."

29

"I'll take a plain slice and a beer." I grinned.

"A plain slice?" He teased.

"I am vegetarian," I responded defensively.

"Oh, I see. My bad. I'll have the same." The server scribbled in her notepad for a moment and then disappeared into the kitchen.

"So, what's your story," Nate said.

"What," I responded.

"I usually can read people so well, but you are mysterious, an ambiguous ghost to me...I can't quite read you."

"Who do you think I am?"

"Well, stop me if I am wrong. From what I have gathered, you are a loner. You spent the whole night with me and didn't send your location to a friend. Which is extremely dangerous. I could have been an ax murderer or something." I rolled my eyes. Not finding his joke funny.

"I'm not done. I think you don't have friends, people who have your back. You are long overdue."

"You're full of yourself."

"Still not finished," he stared at me, gathering his thoughts. "You have this look in your eyes like you're always a thousand miles away. I can tell that you have been through a lot. Your guarded." I stared at him in disbelief. "Am I right?" He smiled. I grabbed my bag from the bag of my chair and stood up.

"This was a mistake," I whimpered.

He shot up quickly. "Sorry, that was a mistake. I shouldn't have been that blunt. I'm sorry." I turned to leave.

"Please, don't leave. I am an actor. My job is interpreting characters. I was just trying to understand you. I didn't mean to upset you."

I took a deep breath and faced him. Tears swelling in my eyes. I hung my bag on the back of my chair and took a seat.

"You're right, OK. You are right. You seem like a nice guy, and I think I like you, but you are still a stranger to me. I am not ready to talk about this. And I need you to respect that."

"I get that. We all have things we would rather forget...And for the record, I like you too."

I cringed, realizing that those words fell from my lips with such ease. I blamed it on the liquor courage. I slumped in the chair and stared at him. Our food came and we ate in silence for what felt like an eternity.

Attempting to break the silence, I said, "Can I have your number?" He nodded. We exchanged phones and typed our names and numbers into each other's contact lists.

"So how did you find this place," I asked.

"My parents brought me here after I saw my first Broadway show, The Lion King."

"How old were you?"

"I was seven. The performance was magical. That was the day I decided to be a performer."

"Why weren't they at your performance, tonight?"

He paused. "My dad died in a car crash a few years ago. My mom hasn't left the house since. I guess losing the love of your life does that to a person." He stared off, trapped in the memory. I placed my hand on his. He looked down at it and smiled at me.

"I lost my parents and sister…in a fire when I was young. I never really got over it." Tears ran down my cheeks. He gave my hand a gentle squeeze.

"Well, I did not expect to be crying on our first date," he joked. He grabbed our empty plates and beer cans and threw them in the trash.

"A date," I questioned.

"I only kiss girls in theatres on dates," he laughed.

"Is that how you make a move?"

"Only on girls named Margaret Baker." I cocked my head to the side, confused about how he knew my last name.

"Oh. You wrote it in my phone. See, Margaret Baker." He showed me the contact.

"Your slick, Nathan Roberts," He viewed me suspiciously.

I pulled out the playbill for his show out of my bag.

"I read it in here."

"I didn't peg you for a beer girl." He laughed.

"I don't drink often. Only on special occasions. Meeting you seemed special enough." I stared into his eyes and felt my hand in his. At that moment, I couldn't imagine not knowing him or life without him.

The waitress approached us. "It's closing time."

"We were just leaving," Nathan said.

We rose from our seats and grabbed our bags. He walked over to the register and paid. He hailed us another cab. I told the driver my address which was about ten minutes from the shop. We told jokes and giggled the whole way home.

I don't know if it was the alcohol, but I put my head on his shoulder and said, "I want to see you again."

He beamed back at me and said, "Me too." The driver pulled up to the sidewalk in front of my building. Nate walked me into the building and to my door.

"This is my stop," I said. He wrapped his arms around me, and I placed my hands on the small of his back.

He whispered in my ear, "Goodnight."

I whispered back to him. "Night." I pulled away. He watched me as I pulled out my keys, opened the door, and hesitantly walked inside. I didn't want the night to end. This was the most fun I have had in centuries. I propelled my bag down and kicked off my shoes. I hung up my jacket in the closet. I immediately headed to the restroom and took a relaxing shower. I replayed the events of my day repeatedly. I concluded my deeds in the bathroom and put on a night gown. I sat on my bed and answered some emails on my phone. That's when I noticed the date. It was Friday the thirteenth, a day characterized by misfortune. As a person with such an unfortunate past, I would usually expect the worst. As I reflect on this day in retrospect, a day usually colored with misfortunes brought me the love of my life.

I laid awake that night. I couldn't seem to stop my mind from continuing the incessant train of thought. Nathan was humble and funny and considerate. I told him I wasn't ready to talk about my past and he respected it. He did not push. He somehow charmed me into letting my guard down and made me feel comfortable confiding in him. I tried to pull myself away from my fantasy. This was not true love. He was not my soulmate. Those things exist in the movies and novels but not in reality. We had a great night. That does not mean a proposal and marriage were in our future. I could not deny our immediate connection, the desire I had to be around him. I tossed and turned restlessly. I wondered if I had gone mad and dreamt up the whole night in my desolation. Was I delusional and desperate for attention? I pushed these thoughts away terrified by their possible validity. The sun peered through the blinds. I felt a rush of possibilities flood my mind. It was a new day and for the first time in centuries, I was happy.

# 5. Love Is in the Air

The date is May 15, 2015. It has been two days since I have seen Nathan Roberts. My mind relentlessly lingered on the time we spent together. I wondered if our one encounter was all that lay in store for the two of us. Was this the end of our tale? Was that night as magically as I remembered it? Did Nathan return my sentiment?

I hadn't known him long, but still I missed him. I felt irreversibly changed by his attention and tender affections. He brought to life a part of me I thought was exterminated, dormant beneath the charcoal of my past. Our time together made me realize that survival and living are not synonymous. I was doing enough to get by but failed to take every opportunity in a stride. I was not truly living. I survived for a reason. My story is not over yet, and I need to resume living my life to the fullest to find out why that is. Could a relationship with Nathan be that very reason?

I vowed to myself that I would make my family's sacrifice worth it. I would live for all of the witches who died that day. I wanted to be someone my family could be proud of. I vowed to claim the love Joan lost. I was tired of drifting in my cloud of despair. At that moment, I choose life. I left my apartment that morning with a new vigor and yearning to be a part of the world I had isolated myself from for centuries. My deprecating, dejected form was annihilated. Instead, I carried myself with immense pride and hope for what could be. I walked to my local coffee shop. I passed this café every day on the way to work but never cared to go inside. Why did I need to? I had a coffee machine at home and there I didn't need to interact with the outside world. I was safe in my own personal bubble. I animatedly interacted with fellow customers and the staff.

"How has your day been...Riley," I asked as I read her name from her name tag.

She smiled back at me. "I am hanging in there. So much has gone wrong today. Thank you for asking," she said contentedly. "How are you?"

"I am the best I've been in a long while," she responded. I smiled back at her.

I ordered my coffee and glanced at my watch. I had a while before I had to be at work. I decided to sit at a vacant booth by the window. I sat for a short while alone with my thoughts. I watched how people interacted with each other. I studied a mother and her teenage daughter at the booth across from me. The teenage girl was angry at her mother for embarrassing her on social media. From what I could gather, her mother posted a throwback picture of her that she did not like. The argument seemed so juvenile. Why are we like this? It is a shame that we do not genuinely appreciate the treasures we have until they vanished. I thought of my family. I missed my mother, I wanted so badly to tell her about Friday night. I pondered for a moment, contemplating what her response would be. Would she be happy for me? I thought of Joan and wondered if she would be jealous or even protective. I laughed to myself. They would marvel at modern-day courtships and the uncertainty that comes with them. My thoughts were interrupted by a familiar voice.

"Funny seeing you here." I looked up eagerly. It was Nathan.

"Hey. What are you up to," I asked?

"I come in here every morning. Are you stalking me?" He chuckled.

I laughed awkwardly. "This is my first time coming here. I am usually a homebody."

Nate took a seat next to me. "Well, it seems like fate is pulling us together."

"It certainly seems like it. Maybe our intertwined story is written in the stars. Are you the Ricky to my Lucy," I joked?

"That is an old reference…but I guess so." I cringed. Fearing I gave my secret away. Did he even believe in the supernatural? Was the possibility of me being from a different time even on his radar? I inspected his expression. He seemed to be confused.

"So old sitcoms kept you away from the theatre this long," he teased.

"What can I say. I am a fan of the classics." We smirked at each other.

"Hmm. Is that right? Maybe, we can watch some reruns together sometime," Nate responded quickly.

"Sounds like a blast." *Why did I just use the word blast? Ugh.*

"Well, it is only fair. I brought you into my world for a day. Show me what makes your heart flutter." He charmed.

"I am a teacher. I teach five-year-old children their colors, number, and the alphabet. I think you already know all about that." We chuckled.

"Besides teaching, what is something that makes you happy. Outside of drinking coffee alone and being with me," he joked.

"Umm...I like to write. I journal every now and again. I like to keep a record of significant events that happen in my life."

"Afraid you might forget?"

"It's possible."

"Oh. You are a creative too. Can I read it sometimes?"

"Well, it is kind of personal." I scrambled.

"Come on. You don't have to be nervous. I won't judge it. I used to keep a diary too."

"Why did you stop?"

"I just lost interest one day. I still write though. I like to write music, lyrics, and poems when I feel inspired."

"What inspires you? Well, besides pretty girls in coffee shops."

"Nature, the beauty in the world around me, you can find beauty in the little things, like the way someone laughs or the sparkle in their eyes."

I felt a soft smile stretch across my face. I looked down at my watch, finally acknowledging the time. I hesitate, not wanting to be sucked out of the moment.

"I have to get to work." He stood up and I followed him out of the booth.

"Nice seeing you today," I spoke.

"See you around," he responded as he walked toward the coffee counter. I left the café and began walking to work. I pulled my phone out of my back pocket. I scrolled through my playlist, attempting to find a good song to walk to. The déjà vu set in. I recalled a similar situation that occurred when I met Nathan. I decided to play the song he recommended. Memories came flooding back from our dance after his show. It was a magical night full of firsts. I entered the school building and entered the faculty break room. I was immediately greeted by my colleague, Mrs. Ross. She is an older gray-haired dark-skinned woman with a muscular physique. She wore her hair in a slicked-back low bun, thick coke bottle glasses, and a navy-blue pantsuit with black heels. She serves as the second-grade teacher, who teaches down the hall from my classroom.

"Well, don't you look chipper today," Mrs. Ross inserted. I smirked in response to her accurate statement.

"I am actually feeling pretty good today."

"I think this is the first time I have seen you smile outside of the classroom." I chuckled.

"OK, then I am in a really good mood today."

"Um, hmm. Who's the boy?"

"Why do you assume it is a boy?"

"It is always a guy," she teased.

"Can't I just be happy," I whined.

"Of course, dear. But I have been around the block for a while. You're smitten. This sudden influx of enthusiasm is a boy's doing." I laughed and shook my head in submission.

For the first time, I enjoyed my conversation with my colleague. I usually dread the morning small talk and rush back to my classroom, evading my fellow co-workers. She reminded me of Mrs. Abbott. Like Mrs. Abbott, she is funny and nurturing, and chatty, making other people surrounding her more comfortable.

"Cup of joe," she asked.

"No, thank you, Mrs. Ross. I just had a cup. I just came in here to say hi to you."

"Oh, that boy certainly did a number on you. In the six months I have known you, you squirm at thought of conversating, Miss Margaret Baker." I chuckled at her sentiment.

"What can I say? I guess I am a raging introvert. How is the family?"

"My youngest is graduating from university in May."

"Oh, what profession does she hope to go into?"

"Medicine. She is off to med school in the fall."

"That is wonderful."

"Yes, we are all beyond proud." She beamed.

"How is Mr. Ross?"

"He just retired from his management position and is trying to get me to step down. His head is full of fantasies about a vacation in the Bahamas or Jamaica. He wants to lie in the sun, drinking coconut milk for the rest of his life. Not me, though. He is going to have to pry my pen and lesson plans from my cold, dead hands." She laughed hysterically and I joined in.

I looked down at my watch and realized that I let time get away from me. My students should be back from breakfast in the cafeteria and class instruction needed to begin. My students are young, and I must stick to a strict routine to get them to cooperate. I picked up my bag.

"Nice conversating with you today, Mrs. Ross."

"You too, dear," she responded as I retreated into the hallway. I sprinted to my classroom and stopped in front of the door. I took a deep breath, acknowledging the noise radiating from the room and saturating the air, obstructing the students in the surrounding rooms from focusing on their lessons.

I danced into the room with a wide grin stretched across my face. I walked over to my desk and took a seat. Despite the lack of color in my home, my classroom was vibrant. The walls were a crisp bright orange. It is welcoming and an attention grabber for students. The floors are hardwood, and a rainbow rug covers the reading center of the room. The walls are covered by cubbies and educational posters and colorful signs. Toys and art supplies are packed neatly onto the corner of the room opposing the reading center. There is a whiteboard by my pristine and organized desk. I was proud of my classroom and the impact I was making on the lives of my students. I was almost immediately sucked into the madness. Seventeen five-year-olds were running amuck and screaming at the tops of their lungs.

I clapped my hands rhythmically and scanned the room.

"Sit down," I raised my voice to a high child-friendly octave. My students obeyed the command and took their respective seats.

I sang and my students followed:

"All of our friends are here today."

I went into my bag and pulled out a folder. I grabbed a stack of letter tracing worksheets and rose from my seat. I walked around to each student and handed them a paper. The room filled with silence as they fixated on their work. I walked around the classroom and checked on my student's progress. I helped a few students with the complexities they faced while completing the assignment. I moved back over toward my desk and wrote the alphabet largely across the whiteboard in black marker. I took a step back and evaluated my work and then took a seat at my desk. My cellphone buzzed in my bag. I scanned the classroom to evaluate whether this was a good time to check my phone. The class, was still, occupied with their assignment. I pulled my phone from my bag and read the forefront notification. I received a text from Nathan. He wanted to see me that evening. I blushed, feeling the warm embrace of young love. I texted him back, agreeing to see him. A smile stretched across my face as I placed my phone back in my bag and slumped into my seat. I let my mind wander onto Nate for a second and I sighed, content right where I was in life.

14 Hours Later

I had come back home from school several hours prior. I was sprawled out on my couch watching a romantic comedy and scarfing down a tub of strawberry ice cream. I put on a white and yellow knee-length floral dress with yellow flats. I put on hoop earrings and applied an appropriately dark nude gloss to my lips. I undid my tightly wrapped bun from the top of my head and lightly tugged at my waist-length curls. Nathan was surprising me; I had no idea what was in store for our evening together.

I heard a knock at the door and jumped to my feet. I ran over to my fridge and placed the tub of ice cream in the freezer. I dusted off my dress and shook out my tresses before making my way to the door and opening it. Nathan stood beaming at me in the doorway.

His long lashes fluttered, and his piercing brown eyes stared into mine. He inspected my form.

"You are stunning." I swiftly moved into the hallway, careful to block his view of my home, and closed my door. He leaned against the door frame, drawing closer to me.

"Thank you," I remarked.

"You are beautiful in that dress."

I melted into his ardent affections. "This old thing," I said sarcastically.

"It brings out the warmth in your skin and the enchantment of your alluring brown eyes."

I blushed and pressed my hands to my checks.

"So, where are we going," I said inquisitively.

"Well, it is a little late and I know that we both have to be up early tomorrow," said Nathan. I nodded my head in agreement.

"So, you aren't up for going anywhere," I asked, afraid of the answer.

"No, I still want to spend time with you, but maybe something lowkey. Is that OK?"

"It's perfect," I reassured. He smiled, relieved.

"OK then. Are you ready to go?" I nodded, eager to be taken on another adventure with him.

He gestured to the other end of the hallway, and we made our strides in the directions. We headed down the flight of stairs and exited the building. We walked to Nathan's car which was conveniently parked in front of the building, and he opened the passenger door for me. I slid into the seat and placed my seat belt on. He walked around to his side, got in, and responsibly put his seat belt on.

"So, where are we going," I asked.

He scratched his head and met my eyes. "Um, right here."

I contorted my face in confusion. "We are just going to sit here in front of my house?"

"Well not in front of your house, and we can listen to music too." He cranked on the radio and a rhymical beat infiltrated the air encompassing us. He began nodding his head and jerking his body to the beat. I chuckled at his ridiculous form.

"Oh, you think you can do better."

"I absolutely know I can." I began bouncing my shoulders in unison with the beats in the music.

"OK, you beat me at that dance battle. I stand corrected." He chuckled.

"We can have a rematch sometime, but you can spare yourself the second wave of humiliation and accept that I am the rightful champion," I teased.

"I think, I am going to have to challenge you again," he suggested. I nodded my head and smirked at him. Nathan pulled out of his parking spot and started onto the road.

"How was work?" I cringed at my sorry excuse for small talk.

"Same old, same old," he responded.

"How was yours," I asked.

"Well. My students were well behaved. I mean, my day was dreadfully average. Boring even."

"That is good. Umm, why don't we spice up this conversation?"

"How so?"

"We are going to play my favorite game. Drum roll please." I heeded his command and began musically tapping on the dashboard. Nathan waved his hands for the music to cease, and I stopped.

"20 Questions," he cheered.

"How do you play," I asked.

"We ask each other random questions, to get to know each other better."

"Alright, that sounds like a fun time."

"OK, you start," he said suavely.

"Hmm." I paused to dream up an impeccable question.

"Any day now," he mocked.

"I am thinking."

"Come on. There isn't one thing that you have been dying to ask me?"

"Fine. What is your biggest fear?"

"Hmm. You started with a loaded question."

"You don't have to answer it if you don't want to."

"I'll answer. It just requires a little thought. Uh, I think it would be not being able to make it in the entertainment business." I placed my hand gently on his shoulder and Nathan remained steadily staring out at the road.

"So, what's yours?"

"I have no idea."

"Seriously, nothing scares you?"

"I don't know."

"I just told you mine. You have to spill. It is the principle."

"Umm. I guess being inadequate, unloved, abandoned…The grief girl trifecta." I moved my hand from his shoulder and stared down at my hands on my lap.

"This game is taking a sad turn. Let me lighten the mood. Umm, what is your favorite color," he said.

"That's a tie between yellow and green."

"OK, good choices. But you completely disregarded the best color. The most superior color is blue." I sighed.

"Nope, no one can change my mind on this topic."

"Interesting development," I teased.

"Blue is the only right answer, Margaret." We laughed. "OK, time for your question," he chimed in.

I realized that this was the perfect opportunity to test the waters and feel out his beliefs regarding what I am. His answer could either empower my will to pursue him or cause me to go running for the hills. "Do you believe in the supernatural?" I asked.

"Supernatural," he asked.

"You know, things like ghosts, vampires, werewolves, psychics, witches." He paused for a moment, contemplating the details of the question.

"Yeah, I believe," Nathan said.

"Really?"

"Don't you?"

"I guess so."

"I just think that we would be naïve to think that we are the only highly intelligent species to exist." I nodded and smiled in agreement. "You must think I am a weirdo now."

"No, I am just so astonished by how similar we are. I have the same sentiment."

"OK, my turn," Nathan inserted eagerly.

"What are three things you can't live without?"

"Hmm. My laptop, my lip balm, and a hair tie."

"A hair tie?"

"Yes, I have a lot of hair. It gets hot sometimes." I chuckled.

"What's your zodiac sign," Nathan asked.

"I am a Cancer," I answered.

"I am a Scorpio."

"I guess that means that we are compatible." I giggled.

"Guess so…Aww, you are about to see my surprise," Nathan said. We turned the corner and saw the bright city lights contrasted by the black night sky.

"This is beautiful," I remarked as I ogled at the signs and lights illuminating the city. Nathan motioned over to the radio and played an instrumental piano melody. It was the perfect mood music for a remarkable evening together.

"You deserve the world and I want to give that to you." I blushed at his kind words. He pulled over at the pinnacle of the street. "Alright, one last question," Nathan said turning to me.

"Shoot, ask away," I responded.

"What is your biggest dream," he asked.

"That is a loaded question."

"Fine, I will go first. My dream is to inspire others, to portray a character on stage and reach someone. I hope that people can relate to me, and that I make an impact on their lives. And maybe I can win a Tony Award and an Oscar."

"That seems incredible."

"I can only hope." He sighed. "So, how about you?"

"I don't know. I want to may teach high school students or become a college professor one day. I can teach English and expose children to impactful, influential literature. I want to find love and marry and start a family. I guess I want the average American Dream."

"Sounds like a dream," he responded. I yawned and looked down at the time on the radio. It was 10:30 pm.

"Alright, I am getting you home sleepy head."

I laughed. "This was really nice, Nate."

"I hope it was. Only the best of nights for you."

"Hmm. Do you do this with all the other girls?"

"What other girls?" He grinned.

"Thank you for this."

"For what?"

"For being there for me. And for just being you."

"Something tells me you can take care of yourself, but I am glad you let me." We spent the remainder of the drive listening to the music and marveling at the city. He pulled up in front of my building, turned off the car, and met my gaze.

"Good night, Margaret Baker."

"Good night, Nathan Roberts." He leaned toward me. I placed my chin on his shoulder and he held me in his embrace. He pulled away and unlocked the car door. I opened the door and scooted out of the car, I swiftly walked into the building and made my way into my apartment. I immediately put on my pajamas and slid under the covers in my bedroom. I drifted off to sleep replaying my evening with Nathan.

# 6. Written in the Stars

We continued to meet each other in that café for two months. We had breakfast together every day. I could feel myself falling head over heels for Nathan Roberts. The date was Saturday, July 18, 2015. I called Nate early in the afternoon, and I invited him over to my apartment after his show later that evening. I intended to uncover his feelings toward me. We hung out every day for months but still, I remained puzzled by the unknown label for our relationship. Were we dating? We hadn't shared a kiss since the first date, did that indicate a decision to remain friends? Was he playing hard to get? The questions were relentlessly drifting in my mind. Was he my best friend or boyfriend? I dreaded asking the question, fearing what his possible answer could be. One thing was for sure, we both made efforts to remain in each other's lives.

I looked around my apartment. I knew I was a messy person but did not feel self-conscious about it until now. I had never welcomed company to my home. I spent so much time isolating myself from the world. I became comfortable with my shortcomings and quirks. As I tried to integrate back into this unfamiliar world, I felt uneasy. I felt so out of touch, living in a dystopian city. I began to tidy the apartment, hoping to make a good impression. I washed the pile of dishes in my sink and vacuumed the carpet. I fluffed the pillows on the couch and dusted my bookshelf. I scrubbed the counters and wiped down the kitchen cabinets. I inspected my apartment, content with the work I had done. I ran to my bedroom and searched through my closet for the quintessential outfit. I did not want something too formal or dressy, but also not too simplistic. I required a seemingly effortless outfit that also complimented me. I scanned over my wardrobe, annoyed by my limited options. After about two minutes of searching, I threw on a "Nirvana" graphic tee and a pair of "mom jeans." I slipped on my white sneakers and studied my appearance in my full-length wall mirror. I cringed. I had never studied my appearance for this long before. I looked at myself up and down and stopped at my hair. My curls were not very defined and certain areas were just frizz. I contemplated whether I had enough time to wash and style it. I decided to put my hair in a messy bun. I pulled out a few strands of hair by my ears and finger twirled it with some leave-in conditioner and water. I looked at the person staring back at me in the mirror. For the first time in a while, I felt pretty and confident, comfortable in my skin.

I heard a knock at the door. I ran to the front door, eager to talk to Nathan. I peered through the peephole and saw him. He was dressed in gray sweats and carried a black bookbag and a guitar. I opened the door, moved aside, and gestured for him to join me inside. He walked in and pulled me into his embrace. He looked around, observing my home, and then chuckled.

"For a homebody, your home is not really homey."

"What do you mean," I questioned.

"You know…" He gestured to the walls. "Where are all the family portraits or posters or colorful décor," he teased.

"My home is moody, like me," I joked. I sat on the couch and gestured for him to sit next to me. He placed his bag on the floor and sat beside me.

"So, how was your day," Nathan asked.

"Same old, same old. How about yours?"

"It was bland." I giggled. "Painfully ordinary." I exhaled loudly. "Do you want to listen to music or something less ideal?"

"Actually, I wrote a song for you. It is short but. I really want you to hear it."

"I'd loved to." I blushed.

He tuned his guitar for a moment he steadied his hand and took a deep breath.

"Here it goes…" He began strumming a few chords and softly sang:

*I met a girl,*
*that turned my world.*
*When we danced under the stage light,*
*she made everything just right.*
*She has a sparkle in her eyes.*
*I know I make her happy even when she tries*
*to bury it deep inside.*

*It resonates at the forefront of her pain.*
*Her tender heart drives me insane.*
*Baby, tell me if you feel the same.*
*I don't wanna just be friends.*
*I want to call you, my girlfriend.*
*I never wanted our first night to end,*
*Because our love story*
*is written in the stars.*
*Oh, oh oh it's written in the stars.*
*Oh, oh oh our story is written in the stars.*

He stared at his guitar for a moment, hesitant to meet my gaze. I took his hand in mine and he timidly looked up at me.

"I love it," I swooned. No one had ever written a song for me. His voice was angelic and heartwarming. It was like he could read my mind. I wanted to gauge the label for our relationship and before I could fix my lips to ask, he did it for me. I could listen to him sing for hours on end. He studied me inquisitively.

"So, what is your answer," he asked quietly.

A wide smile formed on my lips. "Of, course I will be your girlfriend." I lost myself in the unending bliss of young love. Any doubt about our relationship, or whether we were right for each other escaped my mind. He placed his guitar on the other side of him. Nate scooched closer to me and leaned in. I could feel his warm breath on my face and the warmth of his body next to mine. I smelled the pleasantly familiar aroma of his cologne as the scent penetrated my nostrils. Our lips touched and it felt like time had stopped, freezing us in this moment. I had no urge to pull away or hide. I was where I was meant to be, besides Nate. He pulled away and I placed my head on his shoulder. He pulled his phone out of his pocket.

"Let's take a picture to commemorate this moment," Nathan said cheerfully. I nodded. He wrapped his arm around me and pressed his cheek against mine. I smiled as he took the picture, elated from the confirmation of our relationship status.

"Can I post it," he asked.

"Sure," I responded.

"Do you have any social media," Nathan questioned.

"No, I never really wrapped my head around that stuff."

"Oh my gosh. We need to make you a few accounts." He laughed.

"What is the purpose of it."

"Just mindless entertainment and instant gratification."

I chuckled. "OK, let's do it." I handed him my phone and he downloaded an app I had heard of but never joined. We created a short bio that consisted of my name, age, profession, and a series of emojis.

"Let me take a pic of you for your profile." I stood up and posed with my hands on my hips. He chuckled and took the photo. He reviewed it and looked back at me.

"Well, you are stunning in person and on a screen. You are clearly photogenic." He showed me the photo.

"You got my angles on point," I joked.

"Don't get all conceited on me now, supermodel," he teased. I playfully rolled my eyes. I sat back down on the couch and placed my head on his shoulder again.

"Do you want to watch a movie," I asked.

"Sure."

"Is a rom-com OK?"

"The cheesier the better." I scrolled through my DVR and streaming platforms hoping to find an old-school movie. A classic, like a movie adaptation of Romeo and Juliet. We settled on The Notebook. We silently watched the film to the end.

"Have you ever been in love?" I blurted out during the opening scene..

"Well, I have been in other relationships, but I have never fallen as hard as I have with you. There's something different about you." He paused, gathering his thoughts. "How about you?"

"You're my first," I mumbled, embarrassed by my lack of experience in relationships.

"Oh, I am living up to your expectations of love."

"You're exceeding them. I am happy we met that day." I sighed.

He met my gaze. "Me too."

"What made you take an interest in me?"

He paused a moment, being pulled back in his memories.

"I could see how tense you were and how you seemed to shut out the world. Most people walk through the city and marvel at performers or the buildings, or signs or the lights. You seemed to shut all of it out. I could tell you needed a friend. I wanted you to know that someone sees you. I felt the need to show you what this city could offer. I honestly didn't expect to fall in love with you, but here we are. I cracked your heart of stone and you resuscitated mine in the process."

"What happened to your heart." I peered at him confused.

"Before meeting you, I was going through a hard time. I had just booked my debut Broadway role and should have been having the time of my life. My best friend, Sophia, she is in the show with me, pulled me out of a dark place. I still hadn't come to terms with my dad's death. My mom and I were on bad terms and I was experiencing a state of depression. I didn't want to be around anyone. I could barely get out of bed. But Sophia didn't give up on me, she helped me feel again. When you bumped into me that day, I saw myself in you. You were carrying the weight of something you couldn't quite shake. I wanted to repay Sophia's act of kindness and help you. And I am grateful that I did."

My eyes swelled with tears. I gave him a quick peck on the cheek.

"I am so sorry you went through that. Grief and estrangement are tales I know all too well."

"Tell me about it," he said somberly. I hesitated.

"It's OK. I am here for you."

I inhaled sharply as tears rolled down my face. I began to fidget with my mother's necklace as I took myself back down memory lane.

"Where to start? Umm, my mother was killed right in front of me. My father and sister, Joan, her name was Joan..." I sobbed unable to finish the thought. He pulled me toward him and stroked my hair. Still, grief-stricken, I said, "They were taken from me and executed. I don't know their last words or what they did in their final moments. Joan was supposed to get married and have a happily ever after but instead..."

Nathan rubbed my back. "Shh...It's OK. You are safe now."

I pulled away from him and wiped away my tears with my hand.

"I don't mean to upset you, but I thought you said your family died in a fire."

I peered up at the ceiling realizing that I would have to lie to Nathan again. Our relationship, like every relationship I build, is resting on a foundation of lies. I could not expose myself to him. If I tried, I may lose him forever. I swallowed back tears. I thought on my feet, a skill that comes with eternal life.

"My parents had a successful, well-known business in our town and a man that owned a rival business set our home on fire with me and my family inside…My mother and I were the only ones who made it out, but she died shortly after from the burns…I made it out unscathed and was placed in the custody of a family friend," I said stoically. Nathan squeezed my hand.

"That is horrible. No one should ever have to go through that. Did they ever catch the guy who did it?"

I pulled my hand from his and stared at the blank television screen. "No, he got away."

"Do you want a glass of water?"

"No, can you just sit here with me for a little while, Nate?" My voice broke.

"Of course, Maggie."

I looked at him suspiciously. "What did you call me?"

"Maggie, short for Margaret. I needed a cute pet name for you. Do you like it?"

I broke down. "I can't do this. How could I be so stupid?" I sprinted to my bedroom and locked the door. I sat with my back pressed on the door. I buried my head in my knees and sobbed. I hadn't heard that name in years. It represented a time in my life I tried so hard to repress. Hearing it resonate on Nathan's lips was jarring. It felt like I was betraying Joan. How could I fall in love, after hers' was stolen from her? What kind of sister am I? Was falling in love with him selfish? Or was I owed an ounce of happiness after centuries of misery and grief? I sat in quiet for about half an hour, before walking into my connecting bathroom and rinsing my face. I observed my expression in the mirror for a moment. Nate must have left by now. I wondered if I scared him off. I decided to face reality and headed back to the living room. He was silently sitting on the couch. I sat back beside him.

"So, I guess we're not at the nickname stage yet." He chuckled.

I smiled. "Umm…I haven't heard that name in a long time. It kind of took me by surprise."

"I am sorry about that. I know that word doesn't change what happened, but I want you to know that you can talk to me about that stuff. I can't change the past but sharing it can lessen that weight in your heart. I know, it was hard to talk about, but do you feel even a little better?" I nodded.

I did feel the slightest bit of relief even though I had to change specific details from the story. I was finally able to express this tragedy to someone and he understands grief.

"I am happy you stayed."

"I thought you may need me when you were feeling better."

"Why are you so perfect?" I passionately planted a kiss on his lips. I pulled away.

"Are you hungry," I asked.

Nathan smirked. "I ordered some Thai food while you were in your room. I got us some 'Tom Yum Goong' because you said it was your favorite during our last coffee date. If my memory serves me right. You were on your way to pick that up when you met me."

I smiled back at him. "Like I said, 'perfect.'"

"It should be here any minute." He laughed.

Like clockwork, there was a knock at the door. Nathan rose from his sitting position and walked toward the door. He peered through the peephole before opening the door. He took the food and handed the delivery guy money from his back pocket. He joined me on the couch and handed me a container of shrimp soup.

"Do you want to watch a show or something while we eat," I asked?

"Sure. What's your favorite?"

"One Tree Hill. They do not make TV the same. Nothing can compare to that show."

He laughed. "I watched that show growing up. I haven't seen it in years. Let's do it."

"Do you remember anything about the show?"

"Not a thing..." He stroked his chin and stared off in space. "Wait I do remember that a few members of the friend group played basketball...and I think there were cheerleaders...Oh, and there is like a new car accident every season."

"Bingo!" I cheered as I raised my arms above my head and clenched my hands into fists.

I opened my streaming service and played the first episode. We devoured the food as we watched. Nathan disclosed witticisms the entire time. He poked holes in the plot and cringed at some of the dialogue. I laughed more vigorously than I have in a prolonged period. I believe that Nathan was invested in the show, despite his too-cool-for-school act. He was too tenacious to admit what I already knew. After a while of scrutinizing, he eventually took my leftovers and situated them in the fridge. He threw away his empty container and reconvened beside me on the couch. He enclosed his arms around me, and I slumped contentedly. We were halfway through the seventh episode of the first season when I realized Nate had descended into a deep slumber. I laid my head on his chest and continued to immerse myself in the life of the One Tree Hill characters before drifting off to sleep.

I dreamt of an idyllic future with Nathan. We seemed to be a few years older. Approximately thirty-five. Our skin had slightly less elasticity and our fine lines and wrinkles were more prominent. He was stagnant, performing in the original cast of a new Broadway show and I was promoted to a middle school teacher. We moved into a moderate size house. It had a contemporary interior design. The furniture such as couches, chairs, tables, counters, and bookshelves were black, and the walls were gray. We had two children, a five-year-old boy named Derrick Roberts, after Nathan's deceased father, and a three-year-old daughter named Elizabeth Joan Roberts after my mother and sister. The children were beautiful, taking the best parts of their parents for their own. The walls were covered in family photos. In the dream, we were sitting at the dining table having a family dinner. We ate spaghetti and discussed our day with each other. It was charming and strikingly enticing. And now that I understood the gravity of our relationship, I decided that I wanted that life with Nathan.

# 7. A Night to Remember

I was woken the next day by the sun peering through the curtains. I lightly rubbed Nate's shoulder. I grabbed my phone from in between the couch cushions. I turned it on a looked at the time.

"It is six o'clock. We fell asleep. You should probably go and get ready for your matinee show."

"Yeah, see you later." He sighed. He cupped my face and kissed my forehead. He picked up his guitar and his bag before leaving the apartment. I decided to take a shower, wash my hair, and get ready for the day. After finishing up in the bathroom, I put on a green tank top and black leggings. I styled my hair with conditioner and gel before placing my hair up in a high ponytail, after diffusing it. I then proceeded to retrieve my laptop from my nightstand and worked on my lesson plans for the next week. Once I finished, I made myself some toast with grape jelly and a cup of green tea.

I recalled my night with Nathan as I ate at my coffee table. We were vulnerable with each other. He made me feel safe and loved. I haven't felt true happiness in so long. He melted my frozen heart. His smile, his charm, it was magic. Our chemistry was electric. He was beginning to feel like my other half. I have always felt like a part of me died with my family, but he made me feel alive. He made my pulse quicken and my palms sweat. I found myself excited for each passing day, because of the possibility of being around Nate. Now I can call him my boyfriend. The idea of finally courting someone astounded me. I finally grasped the object I romanticized my entire life. I could finally claim it as my own.

Back in my time, Joan and I were considered old to be unmarried. There was a lot of pressure to wed as soon as possible. My parents did not adhere to societal norms and told us not to rush into it. Mother always told me to let love happen organically. And my love did not find me back then. It took centuries of heartache for my love story to begin. I finished my breakfast and washed my plate and mug in the sink. I dried them off and placed them back in their respective places in the cupboard. I glanced at the time on my phone. Nathan's show was starting soon.

I texted him, "Break a leg, boyfriend." I remembered that he had set up a social media account on my phone. I went to the app and searched his name. I scrolled until I recognized his face on the profile picture. He had a blue checkmark beside his name accompanied by one hundred and forty-four thousand followers. I knew that he was "famous," but I did not realize how popular he was.

I clicked the follow button and then read his bio. His status said, "In a relationship." Nate's most recent post was the picture of us together. The caption read, "It was the kind of kiss that made me know that I was never so happy in my whole life – Stephen Chbosky." My heart fluttered. He openly shared me with the world. I was familiar with the book the quote originated from. I left a like on the photo and commented, "We accept the love we think we deserve – Stephen Chbosky."

I immediately received numerous notifications about his followers following me. My one follower, Nathan became one thousand in a matter of seconds. I gasped at this revelation. I turned my phone off, ignoring this unsolicited attention. I headed over to my bookshelf and decided to read the book Nathan and I had quoted. I had read it several times before, but his post made me nostalgic. My life and mindset had changed so much in the past few months. I was due for a dose of familiarity. I laid down on the couch and got lost in my novel for a few hours. I was interrupted by a knock at the door. I put my book down and swiftly moved toward the door. Without checking the peephole, I opened the door.

Nathan was standing there with a tall, slender, blonde woman. I tensed, wondering who this could be. Nathan kissed my cheek and my muscles relaxed.

"Hey, Mags. This is the best friend I told you about, Sophia. Sophia, this is my lovely girlfriend, Margaret."

I smiled and extended my hand toward her. "Nice to meet you. Nate has told me so much about you." She took my hand and shook it with a firm grip.

"Hi, Margaret. This one can't stop going on and on about you." We all chuckled.

"I tried to call you and tell you I was bringing Sophia, but I guess your phone is off," Nate said awkwardly.

"My bad. I was busy writing up lesson plans and then I got lost in a good book."

"That's OK. Do you want to go out to lunch with us," asked Sophia?

"That would be nice." I grinned. Nathan took my hand in his as we headed out of the building. We crossed the busy street and approached his small spotless black car with windows as clear as day. Sophia headed to the backseat and Nathan opened the passenger side door, gesturing for me to get in. I climbed into the car and turned around to smile at Sophia. Nathan came around and sat in the driver's seat. I put on my seat belt and sighed contentedly, ready for a new adventure. The car gently pulled out of the parking spot, and we steadily headed down the main road.

"So, how long have you two known each other," I asked.

Nate responded, "We met in middle school at..."

"We met at a community theatre. We bonded in rehearsals and have been friends ever since," Sophia interrupted.

"Aww. That is sweet." I smiled.

"So, tell me about you. What do you do," Sophia asked eagerly?

"I keep busy. I am a teacher."

"OK, what grade do you teach?"

"Kindergarten."

"Oh, how charming. What are your hobbies," she asked persistently?

"I like to read."

"That is great in all, but you seem so wound up. So uptight. No offense. I am just trying to figure you out. What was your biggest dream as a child?" I paused, inhaling sharply.

"Don't start with this, Soph," Nate protested.

I thought of how I could phrase my thoughts, not intending to reveal the intimate details of who I really am. "I loved leading; I was sort of a natural-born leader. And I wanted to help people however I could. I don't know, maybe a motivational speaker or a poet."

"Now we're getting somewhere." She sighed. "So, why did you give up on that."

Nathan pulled the car aside and then the motion ceased. I could feel him staring at me, but I kept my gaze in front of me. I could tell he was afraid of what my reaction to this interrogation might be.

"I guess life got in the way. I was forced to grow up pretty quickly…"

"That's the thing though. You are still young. As your new friend, I say this with nothing but love. You have so much life to live still. It is too early to settle. Chase your dreams, girlfriend!" I laughed. Sophia was both correct and fallible. I indeed have so much life left to live, but I am not young or naïve. I have seen the cruelties and injustices of this world. I have lived through countless wars and tragedies. I cannot just turn all of that off. That stays with you like a permanent stain on your soul, forever tormenting the host body.

"Isn't she amazing," Nate said to me. I nodded.

"You are always trying to fix someone, Soph. Inspiring people to be their best selves. I was nervous for a moment there, but my two special ladies are getting along."

She stared at me deliberately for a few seconds. "Yeah. I like this one." Sophia smirked. "I know that I can be intense sometimes. I am an extrovert. I live for social interaction. It charges me up." She laughed.

"Alright, knuckleheads. Let's eat." He removed his key from the ignition and step out of the car. He closed his door behind him and walked around toward me. He opened my door and waited for me to climb out, then closed the door behind me.

"Forgetting someone," Sophia teased.

"How could I forget you? You never stop talking," he teased.

He opened her car door and she stood up. Sophia playfully punched his arm in response to his comment.

"Rude," she sneered.

"Come on. Let's not cause a scene," he chuckled.

Nate turned back toward me. He flashed me a sincere smile and wrapped his arm around me. He seemed nervous. Was he worried about our trio's dynamic? Does Sophia hate me? Was I not speaking enough? Insecurity was an unusual color on me. I did not like it. It felt unbecoming and childish, but I could not shake the feeling.

I shot him an awkward smile. He speculated my stance suspiciously. It was as if he could gauge my thoughts through my tense demeanor.

"Are you OK," he whispered to me.

I nodded anxiously. "Just feeling a little bit anxious. I will be alright."

He smiled down at me. "You are doing so well. Don't worry about Sophia. She is earnest but I can tell she likes you. Soph loves deep conversation. She even starts getting philosophical after a few hours of conversation. It is just how she is."

"I am having a good time, Nate. Sophia is great."

We walked into a quaint, old-fashioned bakery named Celines's Sweet Shop. It reminded me of my father's shop, my true home. The walls were pale pink and dark wooden shelves, and cabinets covered the walls. The fluorescent lighting reminded me of the fifties. I felt like I was in a time warp as if I walked through a time machine and entered a time when my life didn't have meaning.

"I thought you said we were getting lunch," I asked confused.

"Soph has a sweet tooth and insisted we come here. I hope this is, OK?"

"It is fine. I am just a little nostalgic. My family owned a bakery." I smiled at pleasant memories of my life before my family's untimely execution. "Thank you for bringing me here."

He kissed my forehead. "How do you do that?"

"What?" I pinched my face in confusion.

"You smile despite all of the horrors you have seen."

I swooned. He somehow saw me for me despite the fences I put up around my heart. I could not bring myself to tell him my truth. He only knows a glamourized version of events, but somehow through the deception, he really saw me for me. I could feel him slowly bringing the girl I once was to the surface. We held each other's gaze, frozen in the moment.

"You guys are cute together and all, but can we please order and eat." Sophia interrupted our affections toward each other.

"All right. We are right behind you." I laughed. We walked over to the register and viewed the treats displayed on the counter.

"Good afternoon, what can I get for you guys today," the woman said.

"I will have a chocolate cupcake with the vanilla buttercream frosting and a bottle of water," Sophia announced. She turned to me.

"Oh. I will have the same thing," I said cheerfully.

"What about you, Nate," Sophia asked.

"I will have water."

"You are so boring," Sophia whined.

"We are singers. We really shouldn't be eating this stuff."

"Live a little, man," she prodded.

"I am good," he reassured.

"OK that will be $10.25," the cashier said.

Before Nathan could reach for his wallet, Sophia blurted out, "I got it!" Nate looked at me and shrugged. The woman handed us our food and we headed outside. Sophia waved at us to follow her. She led us to an outdoor seating area. Sophia took a seat across from me and Nathan sat down in between us.

"Oh, let's take some pics with our cupcakes for social media," Sophia suggested. She pulled her phone out of her pocket and handed it to Nathan. Nate sighed as he stood up and I took his seat. We leaned toward each other and acted as if we were about to bite into the cupcake. Nate moved around us, finding a different angle. After staring at the phone for a short moment, he handed Sophia her phone. I moved back into my seat, and he returned to his.

"These are great. Do you want me to send them to you," Sophia asked?

"Sure." I pulled out my phone and we exchanged numbers.

We ate in silence for a few minutes. Sophia mindlessly scrolled on her social media feed and Nate stared off into space.

He said, breaking the silence, "So, our show contract will be up next month."

"Yeah," Sophia said meeting his gaze.

"We are going to have to get back in those audition rooms." He sighed.

"Well, it was nice having a stable job for six months," Sophia joked.

"Yep, back to casting calls." He chuckled.

He turned to me. "Will you still like me when I am unemployed," he said sarcastically.

"Well…" I teased him and his smile dropped.

"I am kidding. I will follow you through the highs and lows."

His smile reappeared. "Me too, Margaret."

"Alright, love birds. I need to go. My parents are coming to visit, and I have to pick them up from the airport."

"OK. Let's go. I will drop you off first."

We threw away our trash and walked to Nathan's parked car. Sophia and I walked side by side and Nate walked ahead of us. Without Nathan noticing, she pulled me aside.

"You and Nathan are so good together. I am happy for you guys."

"Thank you." I beamed.

"You know, he really likes you. I have seen him through other relationships, but he has got it bad for you, girl. I have never seen him fall in love this hard and so soon."

"You think so." I blushed. She grabbed hold of my shoulders and gave them a gentle squeeze.

"I know so. You're all he talks about." I smiled at her sentiment. "But he needs to know that you feel the same. He is my best friend, and I don't want to see him get hurt. You're so guarded and that will be the downfall of your relationship." My expression hardened.

"I have my reasons," I scorned.

"I am sure you do but that is not an excuse to let this pass you by." She sighed. "Look, I see the way he looks at you, the way his eyes linger when you look away, the way his face lights up when your near or when he talks about you. I can tell you're not a share your feelings type of gal, but I think you will be fond of his response. Don't be afraid to tell him how you feel."

Sophia loosened her grip on my shoulders, and we caught up with Nate. We sat in the same seating from earlier and he pulled out of the spot. We started on the road. We sat in silence for most of the drive.

"So, this has been fun," Sophia said.

"Yes, we should definitely do this again," I agreed.

Nate pulled over in front of a two-family brick house.

"Thanks, man." Sophia leaned forward and hugged him from the back. She pressed her cheek against his.

"Later, Soph." She pulled away.

"Nice meeting you, Sophia."

"Nice meeting you too," she called out.

Sophia got out of the car and walked swiftly toward her house. Nathan pulled away once she stepped through the door.

"So, I heard your conversation with Soph, and I don't want you to feel pressured to say anything before you're ready."

"You heard that?"

"Yeah. Uh…She was right about how I feel about you, but if you are not ready to verbalize the feeling out loud then we don't have to," he said in one breath.

"Oh! Umm…Are you ready to tell me anything?" I said timidly.

He turned on the radio and in a fantastic switch of fate, our song played on the radio. He gasped and then proceeded to grin at this revelation. I think he took it as a sign to tell me how he felt. He took a long inhale.

"I love you. I am not just in love with you, I love you. Love you so much that I feel like my heart may burst. I love your smile and your laugh and how you can get lost in a book and how you make me feel seen and special in one of the most congested cities in the world."

My heart melted. Unable to verbalize how much he means to me, I said, "Dido." He laughed.

"I proclaimed my love for you and all you have to say is 'dido.'"

"What do you want me to say," I snickered.

"I don't know. Maybe, 'I love you too, Nathan,' or 'I feel the same.'" He sighed. "Anything other than 'dido.'"

"I want to say it. I want to be able to more than anything. I am just not ready yet. It's just…"

"…Too soon. It's OK. You can tell me when you're ready." We sat in silence for the rest of the car ride. He pulled up in front of my apartment. I couldn't be honest with him about my feelings because the foundation of our relationship was built on lies. He says he loves me but doesn't know who he is in love with. It wasn't fair to him. I knew that I needed to talk with him. My mind scrambled trying to find the best way to do it. The media portrays an exaggerated depiction of witches. His mind would conjure an image of an old lady with white hair, a humongous nose, and a grotesque mole. He could call me crazy or think I am evil and fear me. My thoughts began to frantically spiral. He tapped my shoulder, alerting me that we reached our destination.

"Can you park? I need to show you something." He nodded and parked the car across the street. We silently entered the building, walked up a flight of stairs, and walked into my home.

He took a seat on my couch.

"Would you like some coffee or tea," I asked softly.

"Umm. Coffee please."

"No milk, two sugars right."

"That would be great."

I headed over to the kitchen. I grabbed a pot from my bottom cabinet. I filled it with hot water and placed it on my lit stove. I pulled two white mugs out of the cupboard. I also grabbed a coffee pod and place it in the keg and poured the hot water into the respective compartment. The coffee flowed into the pitcher, and I poured the contents into the mugs. I added two sugars to each. I slowly walked over to him with the mugs. I handed him his drink and sat next to him. He took a sip and I followed.

"Nate…Um, I think I am falling in love with you. And that terrifies and excites me all in one fell swoop. I want nothing more than to let these feelings overtake me. But I have been keeping a terrible secret. And I can't lie to you anymore. I think I wanted to see myself the way you did that first night, the way you continue to see me. But it isn't real. You don't know the real me."

"What are you talking about, Of course, I know you." I shook my head in protest.

"You don't. You helped me cope for a little while and I let yet you. I didn't expect to love you the way that I do, so I need to be fair to you. You need to know who you are in love with." My voice trembled. Nathan squeezed my hand. I looked away, unable to face him.

I took a deep breath, grounding myself, and returned his curious gaze. "I…I am a Baker Coven witch. My parents were the Coven Regents. And this body and face and voice aren't mine. Umm, I am 341 years old, and I am telling you all this because I trust you. And if you are going to love me, you should know who that person actually is. I don't want this to change things. I don't want you to see me differently." Tears pooled in my eyes and streamed down my cheeks. Nathan was quiet. I turned to meet his gaze and his eyes were wide. His expression was dumbfounded.

"You think I'm a fool, nothing but a bewitched lunatic," I whispered and smoothed my hair back with my hands. He looked at me with bewilderment. He placed his hand on my forehead for a moment, turning his palm and the back of his hand over my skin, regarding the temperature.

I rose from my position. "You do! You think I am mad," I yelled.

He removed his hand from my forehead and met me standing. "I just don't understand," Nate said calmly. "I said, 'I love you,' and you're freaking out. I get it!"

"You think this is a story, a fairytale, dreamt up delusions, the ramblings of a mad man! I wish it weren't true. That this is not my story, my legacy. I wish I could strip this burden from the roots within me, shedding the pain that comes with it."

"You have abandonment and commitment issues. But you don't have to worry. I am right here Mags. I am not leaving you." He took a sip of his coffee and place it on the table. He reached for my hands, and I flinched.

"Stop trying to help me. I don't need to be saved. I am not a damsel. You cannot save me from this! I just need you to hear me out," I yelled.

I realized that he would need concrete proof. The words that were flowing out of my mouth were impossible in his world. I looked around the room wildly. I grabbed a candle from the center of my coffee table and put my mug down. I had to reawaken a part of myself that had been dormant within me for years.

"What are you doing, Mags," he said softly.

"Just give me a second," I exhaled.

"I am calling an ambulance. You're unwell."

"No, just let me concentrate."

"Is this heat stroke? Are you feeling sick? Should I crack a window?"

"Stop it, Nathan."

"What are you doing with the candle, Mags."

"It's got to be like riding a bike," I mumbled.

"Mags, you're scaring me." Nate was slowly approaching me.

"Nate, stay back. It has been a while since I've done this. I don't want to hurt you."

"Margaret, just calm down and we can work through this. Just, give me the candle, babe."

"Ignis," I chanted.

Nate's eyes grew wide as the candle lit. He stumbled backward. His reality was crumbling. I made his impossible possible. I blew away the flame and place the candle back on the table.

"Don't be scared," I soothed. I walked toward him, and he scrambled backward, seemingly afraid of me.

"What are you," he screamed.

"Baby, I am still me. I am the girl you wrote a song for and danced with on stage."

"How did you…?" He pinched his face in confusion and rubbed his eyes.

"I am not going to hurt you, you are the love of my life, Nathan. Please just let me explain it further."

"I need a minute." He charged toward the door.

"Nate, you promised you wouldn't leave me," I sobbed.

"I just need some fresh air." He said, turning back to me. He left and I dropped to my knees. I felt as though my entire world was caving in. Revealing the skeletons in my closet and facing his rejection made me feel like my bones were decaying. The one person, I thought I could trust regarded me as a monster, unable to process the foul matter of darkness and energy that resided within me. The person who gave my life meaning may be gone forever. I planted a seed in Nathan, fostering the possibility of a happy future. I planted a seed that would never bloom no matter how much love, water, and sunlight I give it. In revealing my past, I doomed any shot I had at a future with Nathan Roberts.

# 8. I Was Made to Love You

I laid on the floor, desolate, desperate, and hopeless. My love disappeared just as fast as I found him. My bleeding heart was breaking open, oozing over the world around me, shredded to a trillion pieces at the sight of Nathan's rejection. I stayed frozen in the moment for what seemed like an eternity. Two hours must have come and gone, and Nathan remained distant, gone with the wind without an explanation. I was a paranormal freak in his eyes, a monstrous anomaly, that does not belong in his world or his realm for that matter. I heard a loud knock at the door and scrambled to my feet. The banging sound re-emerged and intensified.

Nathan's voice encompassed the air from the other side of the door. "Margaret, I am so sorry. Please let me in, babe."

"Why should I?"

"I just want to talk with you."

"Leave me be," I barked harshly.

"Please. I don't want to scream our business in the middle of your apartment building. I was wrong to walk out on you. I just needed some space for a moment. I am back now and ready to hear you out."

I raced to the door and swung it open. Nathan pulled me toward him and planted an affectionate kiss. Maintaining this form, we retreated into the room. He kicked the door close with his foot. He pulled away from me and sighed.

"Show, me again," he said collectedly. I was in awe. He was willing to give me another chance to explain.

I picked up the candle, concentrated on the wick, and chanted, "Ignis."

Nathan sighed in disbelief. He buried his face in his hands.

"How old are you again?"

"In this life…"

"This life…" he interrupted. He slumped onto the couch. "How many lifetimes have you lived?" I blew out the candle and took a seat next to him.

"I am twenty-two now. I have lived six lifetimes and I have seven more. My family had this elixir made from the Tree of Life; you know like the one in Genesis." His face was pensive as he nodded. "It granted anyone who drinks from it thirteen lives."

"You're like a cat with nine lives."

"Sort of." I giggled.

"So, did your family really die in a fire? Or was that a cover-up story?"

"They were killed in the Salem Witch Trials. The rest of the story is true. They owned a bakery. My father and sister were taken and killed at separate locations from my mother and me. I watched them burn her and then they finished me off."

"Why didn't they just take the elixir like you?"

I shuddered at the question. "They tried. I took a sip and handed it to my mom…And then those vile people stormed my house and took us to be executed." He pulled me to face his chest and smoothed back my hair.

"It is not your fault."

"I know," I proclaimed stonily. "The world wanted to see my family, my coven, witches in general as monsters, but their fear turned them into creatures worse than the ones they feared. I was a teenager, who needed her parents, and they took my entire world from me without batting an eyelash. And the worst part is that no one cares. For so long, I just wanted to scream it from the rooftops. I wanted the world to know what was taken from me…But I can't because I am different. They will only ever see me as a threat."

"You are safe now," he soothed, patting my back. "I know you; you are not evil. I am sorry that I ran out on you. You were being vulnerable, and I should have respected that."

"I understand your hesitation. We don't live in the same world. I couldn't expect you to adjust to my perspective at the drop of a hat. You came back, that is all that matters."

"I will love you to the end of time."

"And I will love you until the oceans are dust," Nate responded. He cupped my face and wiped away my tears. I rested my head on his shoulder.

"So, you have magic?"

"Yes." I laughed.

"Like a superhero?"

"Umm, not quite."

"How does it work? Can you fly on a broomstick?"

"No. I was only taught Earth magic growing up. So, my powers revolve around the elements of nature, wind, fire, water, and earth."

"That's incredible."

"I am a little rusty though. I haven't practiced in centuries." I met his eyes in a panic. My muscle tensed and I cringed.

"The age difference doesn't bother me. It is not really an age difference. You are twenty-two right now, but you have experienced almost four hundred years of life."

I sighed, relieved by his serenity in this trying circumstance.

"So, I think you said that this isn't your body. What do you mean by that?"

"I get a new one, every time I die. I wake up in the body of a nineteen-year-old girl."

"How do you know your nineteen?"

"Well, I can clearly look at myself and see I am young every time, but my parents taught me all about the elixir when I was a young child."

"You don't have to answer this, but I am curious." He squirmed, uncomfortable by his thoughts. "What is death like?"

I paused for a moment searching for the memory. "You don't have to answer. Sorry, that was insensitive," he blurted.

"No, it is not that. I have no recollection of an afterlife. I remember the pain, and then numbness, and then my world goes black."

"Oh, maybe it is because you don't really die," he spoke. I pinched my face not following his thought.

"Your body dies, but your soul doesn't. It is placed in a new body."

"That is certainly a plausible theory. I have never really fixated too much on that stuff. I just did enough to survive until my time runs out. Your love made me want to live life to the fullest."

"You make me feel like the luckiest man in the world. You lived almost four hundred years without having someone to love. You trusted me with your heart and your secret, and I am going to make it worth the wait." We sat in silence for a few moments, letting our thoughts marinate.

"Have you gone by Margaret Baker in every life?"

"Yes, that is where having different bodies came in hand. You just have to look past the body dysmorphia that comes with it," I said sarcastically.

"Mags, that part of your life was tragic, but you have to come to terms with it at some point. Four hundred years is a long novel. You need a new name to start a new story with a new identity. Is there a new age name that you like?"

"I don't know. What name do you think fits me?" I stood up and spun around in a circle.

"How about Evie? I read that it means life in Hebrew. It seems like an appropriate fit."

"I like Evie."

"Margaret Evie Baker has a nice ring to it." Nate smiled at me.

"Thank you for this," I said tears swelling in my eyes.

"Can I take you somewhere?" Nate asked.

"I don't know I feel like I have had enough adventure for a day."

"It will just be us and I think you might really like it."

I sighed. "OK, I am in."

He took my hand in his as we left the building, crossed the street, and got into his car. We sat in silence for about twenty minutes. The weight of our conversation hung over us. Nathan's calmness granted me hope. He had an out, the perfect excuse to slam the door on us and never look back. He loved me unconditionally. I threw him a curveball and he switched courses without hesitation. And I love him for it. He uprooted his world for me. He is better than any shining knight in amour that I could envision. He didn't give up on me or our relationship. I loved him with my whole being and I plan to until the oceans are dust.

# 9. New Beginnings

We drove for roughly twenty minutes. Nothing deep or eventful happened during the ride. We mostly listened to the radio, and I answered emails on my phone. We pulled into a parking garage. Nathan didn't give me any heads up about where we were going. I was blindly following him. I trusted him with my secrets, my life, my heart. He already had every part of me I cared about. I had nothing to lose. He got out of the car, walked around, and opened my door. I stood up and he wrapped his arm around me, pulling me into his benevolent embrace.

We walked together in silence for seven blocks and crossed a wooded area. We stopped in a scenic, picturesque, meadow. It was an ethereal beauty. The grass was lush and knee-high. It was covered in lavender lilies and white roses. We ran through the field together, and he chased me around in circles.

"You're crazy." I giggled. He picked me up by my waist and twirled me around. He put me down and I took a few steps back and charged him, tackling him to the ground. He laid flat on his back, admitting defeat. His laugh permeated the air and brought a wide grin to my face. I ran my fingers through his hair and stared lovingly into his eyes.

"You got spunk, Margaret Evie Baker."

I winked at Nate. I rolled over and stretched in the bed of grass and flowers content with the beauty and nature surrounding me.

Nathan rolled on his side and watched me. "What are you thinking," he asked.

I rolled over and faced him. "About how beautiful this all is. And how much I love you." He smoothed a strand of hair out my face.

"I am glad I talked to you that day," Nathan said, full of nostalgia.

"Me too."

"If we did one thing differently, we might not have met," Nathan continued.

"The butterfly effect."

"Exactly. Plus, you're not even from this time. It is like fate pushed us together."

"Like you said, 'Our love story is written in the stars.'" He shook his head in agreement. "How are you handling everything? Did my life story make your brain combust," I said sarcastically?

"You definitely threw me for a loop, but I am handling it. I am more torn up inside for you. I don't understand how you get up every day and function like a normal person, after experiencing all of that. I would lose my mind. I would definingly be in an institution by now."

"It wasn't easy. I just kept my head down and focused on my career. My work kept me busy. I have worked as a nurse, a teacher, a nanny, and a housekeeper. My goal in each life was to protect my heart, so I avoided making close-knit relationships." He turned to me with a curious expression.

"What made you give me a chance?"

"I could feel in my gut that I could trust you. I knew that you wouldn't hurt me. I don't really understand why? Maybe I was just desperate for something different, the monotony of my day-to-day life was becoming unbearable." I sighed.

He rubbed my shoulder with his fingertips. "I'm sorry that you were alone for so long. I wish that I could've protected you from all that heartache." I took his hand from my shoulder and pressed it to my lips. I moved his hand to my chest, desiring to keep him close.

"My mother got me through it." He looked at me with confusion written over his face. "Don't be confused. She is very dead." I deprecatingly laughed. "But before they took her from me, she told me not to let the world make a monster of me. And I was just never able to shake the image of her, defeated, on her deathbed and desperate for me to take this final lesson and run with it. I carry the weight of her words with me every day. She said, 'Love yourself despite the circumstances the world generates to make me falter toward the opposite, my dear.' I carry those words with me every day."

"She sounds like a wise woman."

"The wisest…and the most beautiful and kindhearted." I closed my eyes, lingering on the vision of her, that existed in my mind. "She gave me this necklace. It was hers." I released his hand and twirled the pendant around my fingers.

"You are the strongest woman I have ever met. Scratch that. You are the strongest person I know. You handle everything with such grace. And you smile and laugh despite the horrors you've seen. It is remarkable. You are the furthest thing from a monster."

"Thank you. Sometimes, it is really hard and you saying that means the world to me." Tears swelled in my eyes. I sighed and rolled over onto my back, staring at the clouds. "Joan would have loved it here."

"Was Joan your sister?"

"Yeah," I said with my voice breaking.

"She was witty, independent, and classy and responsible and organized. Joan would take off her shoes and shamelessly dance through the meadow alone. She was a bit of a rebel in our day. I miss her a lot. Especially since meeting you. I just want to tell her about everything. We did everything together. She was my best friend and the best sister a girl could ask for."

"I have one more thing to show you." He stood up and extended his hand toward me. I grabbed it and he pulled me up. We walked across the meadow. We approached a small river with a waterfall a short way in the distance. Nathan stopped in front of the river, and I followed. He pulled his sweatshirt and white T-shirt off and set them on a large rock behind us.

"Nate!" I blushed as I covered my eyes. "I was born in the late 1600s. I know I am a new age girl now, but I am still a tad bit old-fashioned." He busted out in laughter.

"Nice to know, but I just wanted to go for a swim." My cheeks flushed with embarrassment. He kicked his shoes off and shimmed down his pants.

"Are you going to join me or just watch," he teased.

"I am coming." I swiftly pulled off my tank top, shimmed my leggings off, let my hair down, and kicked off my shoes. We set our clothes on the rock behind us.

"Last one in is a rotten egg." He chuckled. He sprinted to the water, and I chased after him. We splashed around and floated in the water for a few minutes. I felt like I was reclaiming my youth. I forgot about my troubles or worries. We were in our own world, a haven from the treacherous world we were gifted through inheritance.

"Follow me, Mags," Nate called out to me. He stroked toward the waterfall, and I trailed after him. Once we reached our destination, he hoisted me onto the rock ledge and then climbed up on his own. We walked behind the racing water. I wiped my hand over my face, attempting to fling away the excess water from my face and eyes. Nathen stood behind me and massaged my dripping wet shoulders. My heart fluttered and my eyes closed at his touch.

"This is where you can scream. Say whatever your heart desires. The outside world cannot hear you. You're safe, Mags. Scream." He removed his hands from my shoulders and took several steps away from me, allowing me to process his words. I clenched my fists and my muscles tightened.

"I can't," I bellowed.

"You can. You have been holding on to this for centuries, but you never really dealt with it. You buried it. It has been bubbling up all this time. You ran from your grief. It has been hiding at the surface. You can't let go until you face it." He walked over to me and pressed his chin to my left shoulder. He whispered in my ear, "You go this, babe. Shout from the rooftops." He swiftly moved back to his previous position. I inhaled deeply, breathing in the trauma and pain that colored my unnaturally extended life.

"Turn around...I don't want you to see this," I said with composure, fighting back tears. I turned my head to ensure he listened. He faced the rock wall behind us with his hands over his ears.

I turned back around. I drew in a deep ragged breath and screamed aggressively at the top of my lungs. I dropped to my knees, crushed by the weight of my emotions. My anger was all I had for so long. I sobbed uncontrollably as began to have a panic attack. My heart began to race as I started to hyperventilate. My body trembled, unable to process that I was not in danger, but safe and loved. I did not need to have a gate surrounding my heart anymore. I was safe and nurtured and genuinely loved unconditionally.

"Mags are you OK," Nathan asked.

"I...I can't...I...I can't...breathe," I said frantically gasping for air. He ran over to me, fell to his knees, and wrapped his arms around me.

"Breathe, Margaret. You are OK. I am here for you, as long as you need me."

"No...No, it is not...OK," I said, "still frantic."

"Look at me. Come on look at me." I turned my face toward him. He began to breathe rhythmically. "Follow me." I followed him and my breaths steadied.

"Good, slow in and slow out," he said calmly. "Feel the wind blowing against you, your body on the ground, here the sound of my voice, the crashing waves and the sound of running water from the waterfall. You are safe." He studied my demeanor and then kissed my forehead.

"Sorry about that," I said sheepishly.

"There's no need to apologize to me or anyone about this. It was an average response, perfectly normal. You allowed yourself to grieve after centuries of pain and your body didn't know how to process the resurfacing emotions." He exhaled, seeming relieved by my stillness.

"How do you feel?"

"I feel better like a weight was lifted off my chest. I feel at peace," I responded calmly.

"That's great. You scared me there for a second."

"Centuries of death imposes you with a lot of damage, I guess. I am the broken, messy grief girl staining the lives of those around her."

"You seem to be whole from my view." We smirked simultaneously.

"Hmm. Well, the panic attack and screaming fit I just had, seems to scream the latter."

"Still seems like a perfectly human reaction to losing the people you love." I stared into the brown abyss of his eyes and found a home in them. He stabilized me and consoled my aching heart when I couldn't do it myself. I fell more and more in love with him, with each passing second.

"Promise me this is forever," I blurted out.

"If it is forever you want, forever you shall get. Do you want to seal it with a handshake?" he said sarcastically and giggled. I nudged his chest and sighed.

"I am being serious," I said firmly.

"I couldn't imagine my life without you, Mags. I want forever with you too." He kissed my cheek, saturated with salty tears and sea water. "Are ready to go back," he asked.

"Can we sit here for a little longer?"

"Sure. Whatever you need," he said as he smoothed my hair back.

"I think I love you," I uttered as I wiped away my tears with the back of my hand.

"Dido." He snorted. I playfully punched his chest and laid back against him feeling strong enough to take on the world if he was by my side. No whim or perilous feat felt impossible while I resided in Nathan's arms. I knew that our love could battle the most treacherous waves and turbulent seas. I stared off in space, not wanting our moment together to end. We sat in silence for a few minutes drinking each other's presence.

I yawned. "Thanks for sitting with me. I think I am ready to go now." We swam across the river and then proceeded to put our clothes back on. I put my hair tie around my wrist and let my soaking wet hair down to air dry. We held hands as we started across the meadow.

"Hang on a second." He crouched down and picked a white rose. He stood up smoothed my wet hair behind my ear and placed the rose there. I caressed the back of his hand. We interlaced our fingers and walked through the meadow to the parking garage and back to the car. This day was the most memorable in my entire existence. Nathan made my world turn and by loving me, he helped me love myself again.

# 10. Ashes to Ashes

My name is Joan Baker. The date is March 12, 1693. I am a naïve, love-struck twenty-two-year-old. I am full of the endless bliss of love. I found a young witch, named Charles, a love that consumed me and was ready to embark on a new chapter of my life. I woke up that morning feeling indifferent, I didn't know any better, it was seemingly a typical day. The cottage smelled of Mother's porridge. The scent was intoxicating, pulling me out of my slumber, and displacing me from my bed. Margaret was freshening up for the day in the restroom. She was so bubbly and exuberant the previous night, I wondered how she slept through the night. It was her time to take her place as an integral part of the Baker Coven. I was beyond proud of her. We have talked about this moment since we were young maidens, heads full of fantasies and wonder.

I thought of Charles and the brunch that he planned. I pondered for a moment, could this be it? Was he going to propose a betrothal? We were both old by societal standards. The world expected us to tie the knot years ago. I tried not to be pressured by the constraints of society, but I felt like an anomaly, a social pariah. Was I not pretty enough for a man to want to be tied to me for life? I detested this train of thought. I was being hypocritical. This insecure, erratic behavior was something I used to mock other courters for. Now this behavior was coloring me.

I heard the door to the bathroom creaked open and the sound of footsteps retreating to Margaret's room. When the sound ceased. I took her place in the bathroom. I took a shower and freshened up for my anticipatory day. When I finished in the restroom, I returned to my room and began to choose my outfit for the day. I put on a hunter green jacket-bodice and a black petticoat. I wore my hair tightly curled up in a style called the frontage. I left a few stands out in the front and at the nape of my neck. I applied rouge to my cheeks and lips to enhance my youthful glow. I slipped on my chopines and pantoffles over top. I made my way to the kitchen and heard my family talking inside.

Margaret sat at the dining table beaming. I embraced her from behind and wished her luck on her big day.

"You look marvelous, little sister." She blushed at my affections. I swiftly kissed both of our parents on the cheeks and took a seat to the right of Father, who is seated at the head of the table. Margaret sat down beside me.

"Are you meeting with Charles, today," she said inquisitively.

"Yes, we are going down to the town square at noon…" She furrowed her brow and I let out a long sigh.

"Don't fret, Maggie. I will return before, lunch, just in time for your meeting." I adjusted her floral crown and then took her hand in mine. I gave it a gentle squeeze before meeting her gaze and shooting her a reassuring smile.

"Thanks, Jo." Margaret beamed. She shot me a mischievous smile.

Margaret pointed at a vase of white roses in the center of the table. We concentrated on it for several seconds before joining hands.

We chanted, "Resurgemus."

The vase began to hover over the table. A smile stretched across Father's face. He looked at us with immense pride for successfully completing the spell. He applauded our efforts before returning to his reading. After keeping the vase in the air for a minute, I gave her a nudge. Understanding my gesture, she concluded the spell.

She chanted, "Retornen."

Mother gestured to me, and I rose from the table to assist her in serving the porridge. I did not realize the blessing I had until it was gone. Losing the people, you hold dear in your life, puts things into perspective. I am annoyed at the trivial things I fixated on. I am frustrated by the things I never said or did in the moment. You expect to have more chances, and more time, but that is not always the case. At least, it wasn't for me. Mother took a seat to the left of my father, and I returned to her seat next to me after we served the meal. We blessed the food before consuming it. We discussed our plans for the day as we ate. The morning was quiet, and the air was still. Knowing what I know now, today could have been the best day of my life. This was the quiet before the treacherous storm.

I heard whispers of the Witch Trials in Salem but never believed it to be true. We believed it was a ploy to scare witches into hiding. My parents taught Margaret and me that being a witch was something to take pride in, not a catalyst for fear and destruction. The Trials were a rumor, and we were ignorant.

"I plan on going to the market tomorrow," Margaret said whilst shoving a large spoonful of porridge in her mouth. "Would you like to come with me?" She muttered with a full mouth.

"That sounds splendid! I would love to attend. What are you going for?"

"I need to purchase silk for Mother's birthday dress."

"Does it have to be made from…" I was interrupted by nearby shrieks. Father met our eyes and place a long figure over his lip. He motioned at us to be silent. He swiftly approached the window and smoothed back the curtains to see the neighborhood in ruins. Men with large rifles were kicking open doors of select houses and setting them aflame. His skin paled. Father, shivered as he closed the curtains. My mother gasped at his response, recognizing his change in character and demeanor. This signaled that trouble was afoot and we needed to be prepared for the worse. He turned to meet our gaze.

He took a deep breath and commanded, "Joan, run to the lair now and get the Elixir!" My eyes widened at this request. I learned about the elixir through the coven. I knew what this meant. Father believed we would die. How do you fight a battle without hope? He created a contingency plan before the sky could fall on us. It was witty and terrifying at the same time. I was not ready to die, I still had so much life to live. I was so young, there were infinite possibilities within my reach. Each path was vanishing before my eyes. I knew that even if we managed to trick whoever was enacting this massacre, life would never be the same. How do you carry on with life after living through that? How can you reintegrate into society and act "normal?" Why should we be forced to hide or die, to alleviate their fears?

I cried, "Yes, Father." I swiftly ran back into the hallway, down a flight of stairs, and into the basement. I pried open the crypt door with a lever and I stared at Father, confused by his demeanor, and entered the lair. I frantically went through the shelf of potions until I found the image of the one, I studied. I recognized its pale pink glow and the curved glass bottle. I hurried out of the lair. I placed the bottle on the floor and took a deep breath. I pressed my hands to the door and sealed it with an enchantment. I placed an illusion spell that Father had taught me the day prior. The crypt would look like a normal wall. My ability was not strong enough to hold it long. I estimated that it would last about an hour. I sigh satisfactorily because it might have been long enough to divert their attention. I retrieved the bottle from the floor and headed upstairs.

A selfish thought reared its ugly, intrusive head in my mind. I needed to take it while I could. Who knew how much time we had? I was scared and wanted to live. I wanted to be Edward's bride and go on whimsical adventures. My story couldn't have been over already. The world cannot be that cruel. This is a low moment, but it cannot be my family's end. I had faith that God or some divine force would intervene. I stopped in my tracks uncorked the bottle and took a sip. I braced myself, expecting to feel as though my skin were on fire or a tingling sensation, but nothing happened. I questioned if I grabbed the right bottle or if the Elixir of life was an elaborate myth. I realize that I did not have time to loiter in the hallway. Decisions needed to be made. The Witch Trails were real, and people were dying. I raced back into the kitchen and handed the elixir to Mother.

Father whispered, "Did you seal off the lair with the protection spell?" I nodded.

Mother said, "Let Margaret take it first." She placed the glass bottle in her hand. Joan hesitated and I locked eyes with Father. Was she ready or strong enough for this? Could Margaret handle immortality and the fight for survival? I turned my head as Maggie took a sip. Ready or not this was real. Immortality was rearing its ugly head. Margaret handed the elixir to my mother as our front door came crashing down, along with our innocence and hope for humanity.

Six men dressed in black with firearms entered our home. Father walked toward them with his hands in the air, to establish peace. They did not care for his show of good faith. Those men saw red and would not stop until the witches were exterminated from the Earth. They wanted a war one of the witches, weren't prepared to fight. They attacked us in our homes, and our safety nets, and violated our basic right to life. They shot us while our backs were turned, dealing with the highs and lows of life. They were tainted, corrupt by their fear of the unknown, and uncontrollable.

"What is the meaning of this intrusion," He questioned.

A tall muscular man met Father's gaze and yelled. He was full of anger. His fists were clenched, and he remained stoic. His stance was defensive. He had one goal, kill the abnormal.

"We are cleansing this land of vermin."

Mother hid the vial behind her back. The same man noticed Mother's stance and approached her. He grabbed her by the waist and pulled her body close to his. Father cringed. His face turned red with fury. He violated her personal space and objectified her just to prove that he could. He was on a power trip. This was a game for him. He wanted to see us flinch, to fear for our lives. I prayed that Mother wouldn't give him that satisfaction.

The man whispered in her ear, "Turn around slowly for me love." She did as he commanded. The mysterious liquid in the glass bottle confirmed their theory about us. We were unredeemable monstrosities in their eyes. We were not precious human lives worth preserving. He snatched the vile from her hands and threw it into the fireplace, I watched the hope dim from my mother's eyes as the flames engulfed it. I felt choked. My hope was fleeting.

The man commanded, "Men, dispose of the freaks."

They restrained us with copper handcuffs. This element stung our skin while interfering with our magic. They marched us out of our home. We were instructed to stand still as they burned our home to the ground. I watched tears fall from my parent's eyes as the happy home they built turned to ash. The men began to take us in different directions, splitting us up. I was overcome with grief, acknowledging, that my world was being torn apart. My parents were going to perish, and I would live on in a new body.

I wailed, "Please. Do not do this! Let me go!" I struggled in their arms. I fought to get to my parents, to give them one last kiss or hug goodbye. They had more to teach, more to say. I was not ready to live in a world where they didn't exist. My dad needed to walk me down the aisle someday and my mother needs to reassure me when I feel like I am failing to live up to the standards society places on a woman. I need their love and compassion and graciousness to get me through my extended existence.

My father sharply turned toward me and yelled, "Be calm! Do not let them take away your dignity! We love you!" My eyes swelled with tears. A man placed a bag over my head and lead me away. I was in the dark, isolated from my family, marching toward a temporary death. We walked for a while. My whole body shook fearing for the lives of my family and friends. My palms and armpits began to sweat profusely at the thought of losing the one I love. We walked for a long while under the temperamental sun. The copper cuffs burned my wrists, and the sun scolded my skin. The air grew thick with smoke. It became harder to breathe. My magic was weakened, and I was outnumbered and defenseless. What was the point of trying to retaliate? The cuffs loosened and I felt a person forcefully place my arms around something behind me and then the searing pain returned. The cuffs were replaced. I gasped from the pain. I could feel my skin becoming raw and smelled the scent of burning flesh. I wanted to panic, to scream at the tops of my lungs, but I did not. I remained stoic and composed. I remembered Father's earlier words and allowed them to take root inside of me, anchoring me to my resolve. They would not get a rise out of me. I could not allow them the satisfaction. I will remain dignified to the end. I will not give them the thing they crave the most, hysterics and overwhelming fear. A round, pale-skinned man with a dark beard dressed in an all-black removed the bag from over my head. I held his image in contempt. I pitied the fool who felt so threatened by the unknown, that he sought to exterminate us into extinction.

I recognized a nearby voice pleading for their life besides me. I curiously crooked my head to the right, following the sound, and saw Charles tied to a stake. He looked like he had seen a ghost, terrified by his circumstances. My heart broke for him. He was pale, sweating, and shaking uncontrollably. His eyes were wild, scanning his surroundings desperate to find a way out of the situation.

"No! No! No!...Charles," I called out. He sharply turned his head to me.

"No. They got you too," he shouted. I shook my head in disbelief.

He turned his gaze to a man dressed in black in front of him. "I am a person. A child. Please don't do this to us. You are killing God's creation and for this, you will be condemned. Please, we are people," he begged. The man grimaced at him and walked behind Charles. He tightened the cuffs and Charles grunted in pain. He panted and his head hung heavy in desperation and defeat. The man's lips curved into a satisfactory smile. His apathy enraged me.

"Leave him alone," I yelled, desperate to preserve his life. I turned to Charles. "It is no use, these retched excuses for human beings won't listen to us," I yelled.

The man picked up a torch and walked slowly toward me.

I stamped my foot refusing to go down without a fight. "Satan takes root in you. You're his vessel on earth, promoting pain and war, and destruction. I hope you burn in the fiery pits of hell," I blurted out without hesitation.

"Wait," Charles yelled. "You guys have taken so much from me, from all of us, today. Please, find the benevolence or even pity to let me say goodbye to the women I love," he begged.

"I have loved you since the day we met. We were kids, wide-eyed and excited to live our lives. Loving you was the climax of my story and now it ends with you. I love you with every fiber of my being, Joan. Today is the day, I become a man, inviting death, and declaring the depths of my love to the woman I adore. You make my mornings brighter and life more fulfilling and vibrant. You are my partner, my best friend, the light of my life. And how fitting, Juliet to my Romeo. And like them, we will die together and rekindle our undying love elsewhere. My world is complete with you in it. And I cannot die before asking for your hand in marriage," he cried.

"Yes, I want nothing more than to be your wife!" I said as tears streamed down my flushed cheeks. "I cannot say goodbye to you, Charles. I cannot," I cried.

"Then let us not say goodbye. Good morrow my love."

"Good morrow," I sobbed. "Our wedding would have been lovely," I said as my voice broke.

"You would walk down the aisle in a stunning white dress, like the fairest maiden, this city has ever seen. I would begrudgingly wear a suit, like the perfect gentlemen." He giggled.

I laughed. "There would be white flowers everywhere and our entire families and all of our friends would be in attendance. It would be a marvelous occasion." I sniffled, choking back the influx of tears.

"I, Charles Roberts, take you, Joan Baker, to be my wife, to have and to hold from this day forward for better or worse, for richer, for poorer, in sickness and in health, to love and to cherish…" He swallowed holding back tears…"till death do us part." He smiled as tears rushed down his face.

"I, Joan Baker, take you, Charles Roberts to be my husband, to have and to hold from this day forward for better or worse, for richer, for poorer, in sickness and in health, to love and to…" I rolled my eyes, anticipating the sexist phrase that I was about to complete in honor of the blessed sacrament. "Obey…" I cringed, afraid to say the next part.

"It is OK," He mouthed to me.

"…till death do us part," I cried.

"It is OK, love. We will be reunited one day, possibly in another life and our love will be stronger than ever and we will pick up where we left off."

"That's enough!" A man with a torch swiftly approached. I ignored him staring into Charles's eyes.

"Ashes to ashes," I said.

The man threw the torch at my feet. The fire quickly spread through me as I agonized in pain. I yelped and screamed as the fire engulfed me. I was terrified of death, although mine would only be temporary. I still felt a sense of finality. My life as I knew it was over. The pain was agonizing, melting the flesh from my bones. I prayed that I would lose consciousness and the pain would cease. I kept my eyes on Charles, allowing his face to be that last thing I speculated on in this life. While looking into his green eyes, the pain felt tolerable. I knew I could get through any feat with him, my unofficial husband, by my side, even death herself as she taunted and caressed us. Death could only graze me for now, but Charles would fall victim to her tantalizing charm as she pulled him into her all-consuming embrace with her blinding white light and serene illusions. His eyes flooded with tears as I burned alive. He said one last thing to me before my world went dark.

"Dust to dust…rest easy my love."

# 11. Dust to Dust

Like a phoenix, I rose from the ashes.

I awoke in a panic several hours later, terrified by the events of the day. I hoped it was a bad nightmare that I had awaken from. I was cold, nude and the skies were dark. My mouth was dry, and my body ached. I noticed that my skin was slightly lighter, and my legs were longer. My body, a mere vessel for my soul, felt strange like it didn't belong to me. I felt like a thief in the night, coveting goods that were not mine for the reaping. I was thinner and taller and paler.

I lost my sense of identity. It is jarring, having a mental depiction of yourself for your entire life spontaneously altered. The limbs and torso I see are of a stranger.

I was eager and terrified to see the reflection of my new face. I did not want to be vain, although the selfish thoughts reared their ugly head into my consciousness. I need to be grateful, and appreciative of the new life bestowed upon me. So many others had lost that. I pushed all thoughts of appearance away from my mind. I was ignoring an important piece of information, the elixir worked. This meant that Margaret was alone and alive somewhere out there, reeling from the effects of this horrid day. That also meant that my beloved parents, the reason I had any chance of survival, were dead. I would have to continue without them.

Another heartbreaking conclusion edged its way into my mind. Charles was dead. He watched my execution and waited for his turn. I gasped and covered my hand with my mouth. He probably died believing that we would be reunited in the afterlife. He might have hoped that our fairytale would continue in another realm. That would have been lovely, but it would never happen. I am here, walking among the angels and demons that roam the earth. Unfortunately, today the demons won. The angels are crying in a corner with their wings clipped, unable to swarm the sky.

The witches have been backed into a corner, forced to hide for the foreseeable future. The world is not ready for us. We cannot live in harmony with the mortals because they will always fixate on the things that make us different. In their minds, I am one of two things, a liability, or a weapon.

Those unrelenting, power-crazed people took Charles and my parents from me. He made my sister and I estranged from each other, clinging to our unnatural newfound lives. They tried to kill me and Margaret. But we are still alive and kicking, readying for war. They started it but I was wholeheartedly prepared to end it. I wanted to wreak havoc on them, giving them a taste of hell on earth. I wanted them to suffer the way I did. They needed to hurt, and I wanted to be the one to stick the knife in their backs and watch them bleed.

I thought of the way they defiled my mother and how they handled and marched us to our deaths. I recalled the searing pain of the magic dampening cuffs. I remembered the powerless feeling they gave me, the fear in my heart. The face my sister made as they took me away. I recalled her screams, cries, and pleas for help. No one could help, we were vulnerable, trapped in a hopeless situation for no good reason.

Today is the day she awoke to the world and understood how cruel it could be. I saw the mental shift when the door to our home came crashing down along with the ringing melody of the screams of our neighbors, she wore her fear-like perfume and the men found this scent appealing. I wore mine as a stench, disgusted by how far humanity has fallen. We were meant to be these compassionate stewards of the earth. We took that dominion and used it to hurt each other.

I wanted blood, an eye for an eye. I grieved, not only for the lives lost but for my sister's childhood, her sunny disposition, and her positive outlook. She was the living breathing embodiment of purity and the just-world phenomenon. They made her grow up on their terms. I feared what this event might have turned her into, would this break her? Can she survive this? Will adversity swallow her whole or will she rise from the ashes with me, dusting herself off and engulfing the flames within her. Does her hurt burn the way mine does? Will she convert to a loaded arsenal with me, a ticking time bomb, prepared to fight for the lives of all those lost? I was mentally readying the metaphoric gasoline and matches.

Those men forcefully entered my sanctuary, wanting to find, the wicked, monsters that roam the earth. I was prepared to give them hell, their attempt to subdue my people was cute, nothing compared to the horrors I could inflict.

These thoughts consumed me, igniting a fire in the pit of my stomach. My anger flourished and my body violently shook. I did not let myself cry over my tragedy. I could not give them the satisfaction of making me sweat, of making me shed a tear. There was work to be done. I needed to remain dignified and handle my reality with grace. I brought my knees to my chest, hugged them, and buried my face in them. I need a moment to compose myself. I took a deep breath, readying myself for the long battle ahead. I needed to be strong, to tear down an empire with such deep-rooted unyielding hate. I stood up and scanned my surroundings. There were no clothing or tarps or blankets around me. I panicked momentarily as I raced to find a method of covering myself. I was forced to turn to nature. I spotted a Hydrangea bush about half a mile to the left of me. I gathered the flowers and made two bouquets, covering my chest and groin area as I walked to find shelter. I could not bring myself to think about Charles and our last conversation. I had one immediate goal, survival. I walked along the woods to avoid being seen. I knew I had to find shelter before sunrise because the killing spree would resurface.

I found an abandoned hovel at the edge of town. I put the hydrangeas on the ground beside the door so my hands would be free. I looked at the door and assessed my surroundings. I found a rock a few paces away from me. I walked over and picked it up. I tossed it around in my hands as I plotted my course of action.

I broke the lock off with a rock and forced my way in. I investigated the property, carefully not to make any noise, as I searched for a sign of other inhabitants. The hovel was quiet and still. No one was home. I wandered into a plain bare-walled bedroom. The décor was almost nonexistent. There was a trunk and a small cot in the room on opposing sides. I opened the trunk and found men's clothing.

I picked out a pair of trousers and looked at the waistband. I held them up to my new body, and examine my figure to the waistband. They were going to be a little big on me. I left the room hoping this mysterious man, had a wife or child around my age. I walked to the end of the small hallway and found a pale pink room. I had a dark metal trunk and a small cot at the opposing ends of the room. This room, however, had a small, beat-up teddy bear on the make-shift bed. I walked over to the trunk and opened it, revealing dresses for a toddler child. I concluded that a single father and his daughter lived here and fled for an unknown reason. I sighed annoyed by my lack of options. I scratched the back of my head, attempting to find a resolution. I noticed that my hair was now shoulder length, as opposed to the previous waist length.

I slammed the trunk close and rose from my position. I exhausted my options. I needed to wear the men's clothing and masquerade as one until I could obtain the appropriate funds to purchase fabric from the market. I retreated down the hall, entered the room, and opened the metal trunk. I put on the black trousers that I had seen before. I rummaged deeper in the bin and found a white button-down top. I draped it on my shoulders and slid my right arm and then left arm through. I straightened my collar and then buttoned the shirts from top to bottom.

I continued to search through the trunk, hoping to find more. I discovered a standard black top hat and a gray wool jacket. A floorboard creaked as I turned to exit the room. Curious about the hidden gems that may live underneath, I knelt on the floor in front of it and pried the plank of wood up with my bare hands. Without expelling much effort, the plank gave away, lifting from the floor. I placed it beside me on the floor and peered into the gaping hole in the floor. To my surprise, a plethora of grimoires was hidden under the floorboards. I carefully reached into the abyss and placed each grimoire on the floor next to me. There were forty-seven brown leather books with the family name. "Dunford" stitched across the binder. Armed with this information, I concluded that the family that used to live here had some sort of insight into the Salem Witch Trials and fled before they could be captured and executed. I skimmed through a few of the books and was in awe at the complexity of the enchantments. Indoctrinated by my father's love for learning, I read all of them cover to cover.

I was only taught earth magic but there was a variety of magic types that I never heard of. This information empowered me. I had the ability to alter the world in ways I had never imagined. I read about the theory of reincarnation.

The book claimed that a person with unfinished business in this life may be reincarnated. I thought of Charles, a young man with so much life left. This revelation gave me hope that we would find each other again. Maybe in another time because our story is not over. It can't be. I continued reading and found a soulmate locator spell. If my love for him remained true, we would find each other again. I needed something of his. I found some straw on the floor next to me. I must have tracked it in the house from the woods. I picked it up and twisted it around my left-hand ring finger. I did not have anything of his, however, this ring symbolizes something of his I wore on my sleeve, his vow to love me. I closed my eyes and took a deep inhale; I had not allowed myself to feel the intense weight of the many emotions of the day. They were starting to weigh down on me. I slumped against the trunk for support. If there was a possibility of Charles being reborn, I needed a way to find him. I reread the instructions in one of the grimoires. It is said to establish a connection to the person you want to find. I focused on my memories of him and the way he made me feel. My mind flooded with memories from the day we met.

* * *

We were seventeen, finishing our schooling and dreaming of our futures. We met at a coven meeting; I had attended the meetings my entire life, but Charles was new to town. His family chose to join my parents' coven. Our meeting took place in the lair of my childhood home. I was sitting outside, waiting for the guests to arrive and the meeting to start. I was reading a Shakespearean Tragedy. I was engrossed in the material, captivated by the story of Hamlet, a juvenile gentleman tasked by his deceased father with righting the wrongs of his uncle.

I was interposed by a teenage boy standing over me.

"Hello, fair lady. Is this a Baker Coven convention?"

I gawked up at him, curious about the unfamiliar boy in my presence. He had fair skin, rosy cheeks, a slender, lanky frame, and dark brown hair.

"Yes, it takes place in the bounds of the hovel. Just follow your instincts. Sense the trail of magic around you and adhere to it."

"Thank you. My name is Charles, Charles Roberts. My family journeyed to this land a week ago. We hope to smoothly integrate into your community."

"I'm Joan, Joan Baker." I giggled, teasing his atypical utterance.

"What are you studying, Joan?"

"Only the most brilliant poet and playwright of our time."

He examined the cover and spine of my book. "Ah, you like Shakespeare, a classic. You have good taste."

"Have you read, Hamlet?"

"Yes. It is a marvelous and enticing story about the irrationality and delusions of a man, while also juggling the concepts of greed and a lust for power. It is truly a work of art." I was aroused by his intelligent observation.

"That was the most poetic synopsis of this composition I have ever perceived. You have a way with words."

"Thank you. I hope I do not sound coy, but I find your beauty to be entrancing." I blushed and he sat down beside me.

I snubbed his advances toward me. "How are you finding Salem?"

"It certainly is quaint compared to my posh homeland."

"Where are you from?"

"I was born in London and spent much of my childhood there. My father is a traveling merchant and his work brought us here."

"How long will you be staying," I questioned.

"As long as my father has work." We sat awkwardly in silence for a few minutes. I twirled my hair air around my finger and stared off into space. I could feel the attraction and connection between the two of us. I questioned if I even wanted to court someone or even have a husband. I couldn't delineate that for myself. Tactlessly, it was envisaged in society at the time. Women anticipated being homemakers, mothers, and wives whilst the men got to have fulfilling careers. I fancied that for myself. I desired to voyage the world and pursue higher levels of education, maybe write literature that people will marvel at for centuries. I could not say this aloud. The world would ogle at a woman for verbalizing these thoughts, let alone bringing them into full fruition. They would claim that it was against femininity or the unspoken laws of attraction. They would call me unwomanly and ostracize me for having unnatural desires. Even if I wanted to speak up and walk to the beat of my own drum, the world already set limits on my freedom. Who would hire me or listen to the stories I tell, or permit me to buy the property of my own? Without a man by your side, you are doomed to misery as a woman in this time. Women are property passed from one man, our fathers, to another, our spouse. Who you marry affects the course of the rest of your life? Will it be lavish or a struggle? Will you feel loved and respected or commanded like an animal in need of domestication?

"My preferred preoccupation is riding," he said.

"Like a horse-drawn carriage," I said puzzled.

"No, bareback, roaming carefree along the road. There is truly nothing quite as liberating."

"Ah, I see are you a trained rider."

"Yes, an equestrian. I used to compete back in London."

"How wonderful?" I marveled. "Do you have horses here?"

"Yes. My family owns a stable about half a mile from here. Would you like to accompany me?"

"I would be delighted." I smiled warmly. He stood up, held his right hand with his left, and stuck out his elbow. Following his lead, I stood up, dusted off my dress, and interlaced my arm in his. We took off into the distance.

"Tell me about yourself," he said curiously.

"What would interest you?"

"What is your life like?"

"I study magic. I align with the coven, beautifying the neighborhood."

"I am mastering the craft as well. I hope to use it to succor the public, actively saving lives."

"I as well. Nothing would make me happier." A wide grin stretched across my face, as I smoothed a strand of hair away from my face.

"Divulge with me concerning your family unit?"

"You certainly are a curious stranger."

"I just want to know more about my neighbor and the family coven I am enlisting to."

"Well, in that case, I have a little sister. Her name is Margaret. She is fourteen years of age and goes on and on about being a wife and a mother," I said sarcastically.

"Is there something wrong with that aspiration?" He looked at me puzzled.

"No. She would be happy to devote her life to a husband and children. She romanticizes the idea of marriage and having a family."

"Is it not a romantic institution," he asked still puzzled.

"Do not be daft. Marriage is an obligation, a requirement by society. True love does not really exist. It is merely a fantasy, a child's bedtime tale, a driving point in the plot of novels. It does not exist in real life." I looked down at the novel I was reading earlier. "Look at what love and a false sense of hope did to Ophelia. Love left her as an orphan and caused her mental decline and ultimately, caused her to take her own life."

"I wholly disagree. Love is out there. We merely have to look closely for it." I rolled my eyes and Charles chuckled to himself.

I accepted his offer, partially to appease the vultures of society. I was hyper-sensitive to the fact that word would spread if I rejected a male suitor's advances. He was the only suitor to approach me. I wanted a new friend and did not plan to have anything more. Charles Roberts charmed his way through my hard exterior, carving out a special place in my heart that only exists for him. He turned my world and made me believe in love.

"Marriage does not have to be an obligation. If you enter into it with the right person, it can feel like you are exactly where you are meant to be."

"Have you ever been married?"

"Well, no…"

I interrupted his thought. "Have you ever been in love?"

"No!" He scuffed. "But it must be. I have watched siblings fall in love in marriage and the latter. I know love exists. I believe in soul mates, a person made to be your other half, someone that completes you."

"That sounds lovely, but I am afraid it is a fantasy. A soulmate is a story people tell themselves to obtain hope to cope with the constraints and oppression in society."

"You are so pessimistic." He laughed.

"You are a brainwashed optimistic, simpleton," I said defensively. I pulled away from him, turned around, and stomped in the opposite direction.

"Do you even know your way back from here?" he called out smugly. I stopped in my tracks and turned back around.

"Take me back," I demanded.

"Uh, uh. We had a deal, Joan Baker. We must get you to bareback on a horse first."

"We are missing the meeting," I whined.

"Your sister can fill you in on what you missed," he teased. I sighed and gently massaged my temples with my fingertips.

"I will stay with you. This is only because the way back escaped me."

"I do not think so, Joan. I think that you are warming up to me." We continued walking along the path standing side by side.

"How much longer?" I whined.

"You certainly complain a lot," he joked.

"You think you're funny…" My left foot sunk down. I looked down, afraid of what I might have seen. My heel sunk down in a small mud pit.

"No! No! These are new shoes."

"Whatever could be wrong princess? Are you afraid of a little mud?" He laughed.

"This is not funny!" I yelled.

"OK. You are right. This is not funny. A stuffy, prim, and proper princess should not be stuck in the mud." He crouched down and slightly lifted my dress, exposing my ankle. I watched him carefully. He grabbed a fistful of mud in his left hand.

"What are you doing?" I questioned. He rose to his feet quickly and smeared it on my neck.

"Hey!" I protested as I pushed him away.

"Your right. This should be a fair fight," he spoke. He bent back down lifted my dress, exposing my ankle, and wedged my foot out of the pit. He grabbed a fistful of mud in both hands and ran a few paces back.

"You are vile!" I shouted. "What possessed you to do this?"

"You are a little stuffy. I am trying to loosen you up."

"I was mistaken, leaving with you." I turned my back to Charles, readying myself to leave. I felt two blows to my back and slowly turned around. I stomped over to the pit and grabbed two fists full of mud and hurled them toward Charles.

"Now, you are understanding." I rolled my eyes at him. We continued to pelt each other with mud, back and forth. I did not admit it to him in the moment, but I was enjoying myself. He charged toward me and threw me down into the mud. I rolled over and pinned him down.

"Huh. I am triumphant at last." I smirked, I stood up and extended my hand toward him. He shook his head and chuckled as he grasped my hand. He stood up and raked his hands through his now untidy, shaggy hair. I took my eyes off Charles, looking up at the sky. We were starting to run out of daylight. "It is getting dark."

"Fair game. Same time tomorrow."

"You are on." We started back up the path toward my home.

"It's a shame, we ran out of time."

"There is always next time." I nodded. "Wow, are you actually disappointed? The maiden who did not want to accompany me is disappointed by our misuse of time." I looked away from him, defensive and embarrassed.

"The assertive, opinionated Joan Baker is silent," he persisted. I rolled my eyes in a substandard act of defiance. He bested me, but I could not admit it to him. He melted a small portion of my stubborn, icy heart.

"I am covered in mud. I did not enjoy myself. I merely hoped to pet the animals." I scoffed.

"I am getting through to you. I can sense it." He wagged his pointer finger and laughed.

We walked the rest of the way in silence. I refused to admit or even acknowledge how I felt about him. He quickly became a friend to me. Charles was correct, he did indeed get through to me. We met each other almost every day. We rode horses together and journeyed to the market. We continued this way for two years. Our neighborhood whispered about us, wondering when we would tie the knot or even announce our courtship. Charles knew how I felt about courting and societal pressures on a woman for marriage, he did not rush me. He accepted that I wanted friendship although I could sense he wanted more.

* * *

I recalled the day he found the courage to profess his love for me. He took me riding and we ventured to grassland on the edge of town. We secured the horses at a nearby stable. We sat next to each other leaning on a trunk of a tree, absorbing the contents of our novels. Everything was perfect. It was a beautiful spring day. The date was March 1st, 1693. Twelve days from now our stories would reach their final chapter, and we were blissfully unaware. We were young and in love and could not verbalize it. In retrospect, I am infuriated by the time I wasted, obsessing over trivial pursuits, gauging how society would perceive the uncertainty of our relationship. We sat so close that our hands touched, and my heart swirled. Instinctively, I rested my head on his lap, embellishing the moment. He brushed my hair out of my face, and I looked up at him, meeting his eyes. Finally acknowledging my actions, I hastily sat up and scooted away from him. He placed his hand on mine and rubbed his thumb over the back of my clenched fist. I pulled my hand away, mortified.

"I apologize. I do not know what came over me," I said sheepishly. He scooted back over to me, and I cringed, fearing the repercussions of my actions. I have friend zoned him for so long. Did he feel a connection between us too? Would my sudden revelation and actions ruin our friendship? I valued what we had, but did he want more? Was I ready for something more? I had pictured something different for myself, my entire life. I never wanted to be a lovesick puppy dog waiting to be a bride. But Charles changed me. I wanted to be his bride.

"I thought I would be the first to make a move." He chuckled. I turned away from him, horrified. "We can just forget about it if you want." I did not want to simply forget it. My heart ached for him, but my mind had reservations. I paused for a moment, contemplating my next course of action. What should I lead with, heart or mind? I would condemn myself to a life of misery, having the thing you want so close, yet so far, if I did not confess my feelings. I was afraid they would swallow me whole if I did not let them flow out of the vessel they claimed. I shook my head, allowing myself to be open and honest about my feelings.

I faced Charles. "I am infatuated by you. I do not want us to merely be friends. We are lovers."

"It took you long enough to realize it." He laughed. Charles brushed my hair behind my ear and caressed my cheek. I placed my hand on his, reveling in the moment. I leaned in toward him and felt his warm breath against my face. Our lips locked and my heart fluttered. I felt like I could float away at any moment and his love anchored me to the ground.

I pulled away. "You know I am not going to shapeshift into the homemaker, stay-at-home Mom kind of girl, right?"

He chuckled. "I would not have it any other way, my love." I leaned back toward him, and our lips affectionately touched once again. Our display of affection was disturbed by the downpour of rain.

He looked up to the sky and laughed. "Well, this demolished our afternoon." I stood up and started to twirl around, gleefully dancing. He followed my lead side-stepping in the rain. He turned to face me and placed his hands around my waist, pulling my body more adjacent to his. My heart rate quickened, and my cheeks turned rosy.

"I love you, Joan Baker."

I wrapped my arms around his neck and smiled, overcome with the bliss of the moment. "I love you too, Charles Roberts." We kissed again and it was perfect, like the kiss of fairytales, like a scene taken out of an iconic romance novel. I shivered and he pulled away. Charles swiftly removed his jacket and draped it around my shoulders. He placed his right hand on the small of my back and held my forearm in his left hand. I picked up both of our novels and he ushered me back to the stable. I sat in his arms on the ground, unbothered by the stench of feces in the stable or my unhygienic, unpleasant surroundings. We cuddled and canoodled, attempting to keep each other warm.

"Are you too cold my love?" he whispered.

"I am perfect, sweetheart. Exactly where I want to be, in your arms." He kissed the top of my head and exhaled noisily.

"I am too," he whispered. I took his left arm from around me. I rubbed his hand with my thumb and then pressed it to my lips. This was a faultless, picture-perfect date, the ones reveries are made of. I wanted to stay in that moment for as long as possible. Charles was my muse, my blind spot, the man I was willing to compromise my previous principles for and it did not feel like a detriment. I was irreversibly in love with Charles and did not suspect our stories next few chapters.

* * *

I pulled myself out of the memory as tears swelled in my eyes and I wiped them away with my long sleeve. I referred to the grimoire, intending to enact the spell perfectly. The spells within it seemed out of my league and mastering each step was crucial. Fueled with the emotions from our first day together, I waved my right hand over the makeshift ring and charmed it to glow when he was near. All I had to do was wait until we crossed each other's path again. I had faith that he would find me, and I would be ready to love him again, ready to be his wife and have his children. The idea of seeing him again kept me sane throughout the years. I traveled the world, looking for him. I worked as a nurse in Salem throughout the centuries. I have not entertained male advances during my existence. I could not allow myself to fall in love again, when the man I wanted more than life itself may find me again. In my head we were married, soulmates, infinitely in love. I wanted to find Margaret and help her through this. I hoped that she toughens up to endure our harsh reality. I wanted her to be happy, with a fulfilling career and an encompassing love. I searched for her for centuries, but unfortunately, I did not have the help of a spell. I did not have anything that represents her or even a physical memento of hers. We were better apart while the Trials were occurring. We needed to keep a low profile until they conclude the executions. I planned to search for her once they were over, but she seemed impossible to find. I guess Margaret Baker is a generic name. How do you find someone without knowing their location or appearance? The Trials took everything but my hope. I had hope for humanity and hope that Charles, Margaret, and I would come together again.

*  *  *

The year is 1864. I was still unsuccessful in finding my loved ones. I lived in London, attempting to feel connected to Charles and hopefully find his reincarnated form in his former home. I brought the collection of grimoires with me, during my travels and read each one cover to cover, studying each spell and interpreting every complexity. I felt like in retaining this aspect of my humanity, I defeated the horrid people whole tried to steal it from me. I lived in a cheap Victorian-style home and lived under the alias of Florence Jones. I mascaraed as a widow of a soldier in the Second Anglo-Burmese War. I worked as a midwife at Saint Bartholomew's Hospital. My work kept me afloat and busy. I was not entirely fulfilled with my career or at peace with what happened to my family. My anger still thundered beneath my composed stature. I wanted sweet, sweet vengeance for my family and my long-lost love. Witches fled into hiding. Our once prideful, booming neighborhoods were now echoing of the past. Witches were scared to practice their craft and the ones who did, practiced behind closed doors away from prying eyes. This made me sick to my stomach. Father would be ashamed of our people for living in fear, denying an integral part of our identities. Our ancestors would recoil at our submission. It made my blood boil. We let our abusers win.

I met a young midwife, Millicent Williams, a fellow fed-up witch, who worked at the infirmary. We spoke in hush tones of our outrage whenever we had a spare moment. She was not alive during the Salem Trials, but she was a product of the aftermath. She heard the tales of the way things were before and yearned for a society that accepted, not oppressed her supernatural abilities. Together, we started a secret, underground resistance movement in an abandoned home on the outskirts of town. I felt at peace, happy to finally be making a difference and uplifting my people.

The coven was open to both witches and carefully vetted mortal witch sympathizers, with the aid of a truth tonic to deduce their true intentions for our kind. Once they were proved to be genuine, we allowed them into the secret inner workings of the movement. There were codes and signals and hieroglyphics that each member had to learn before being initiated into our society. We created a place where people could be proud of being a witch and could learn forgotten traditions and complex spells. I acted as regent to our secret coven, continuing my parents' legacy. We were all motivated by our anger and planned to reclaim our place in society when the time was right. Once we mastered the complex enchantments needed to defend ourselves, the mayhem and destruction would begin.

We would start small, plaster our emblem, a double-headed snake over a cauldron all over the city. When authorities inevitably discovered us, due to our bold declaration of war, we would be prepared to fight to the death. They dishonorably shot us in the back in 1693. This time, we would be ready for a fight.

These plans were vetoed by me after Millicent's death. She was taken by tuberculosis, and I was filled with immense sadness after saying goodbye to my partner in crime and best friend. I was unable to see her during her final days, due to the contagiousness of the sickness. I could not lead with the weight of her death on my shoulders. I refused to continue without her by my side. I mourned her in private, not displaying my vulnerability to the public. I was still at war. I was at war with the people who wanted my kind exterminated and with myself for my inability to find Margaret. She was still alone, grief-stricken, and needing of her sister. I allowed myself to be distracted by foolish pursuits.

I conclude that I wasted too much time in one location. I gathered there to find Charles and hoped that Margaret resided close by since she never spoke of any particular places, she had hoped to visit during our time together. She could have been anywhere in the entire world, mourning me. I decided to put the lives of my family ahead of my unrelenting hatred. A resistance movement was never written in my plan for my life. So, to the people's dismay, I disbanded it and left it behind. My revenge would have to wait.

* * *

The date is March 12, 2016. I am now 26 years old. I am 5 feet 10 inches with ginger straight hair, sun-kissed skin, and an hourglass, slender build. I am single, although I have encountered plenty of male suitors. I still wear Charles's ring as a reminder of our love and my means of finding him someday. I am a writer and have twenty-five published novels. I write under a few pseudonyms so that I could publish over centuries and remain undiscovered. My best friend is my literary agent and editor, Emma Sanchez. She is a well-spoken, beautiful, kindhearted person who has stuck by me throughout this life. She is the only person who knows my identity, my story. She does not push me to find love but instead tells me to go out and see the world. How was I supposed to find Maggie and Charles if I did not search? You may wonder why I trust a random mortal with my deepest darkest secret. I knew I could trust her because she is a witch too. I could sense the magic radiating from her the day she interviewed me after reading my manuscript. This took place about a year ago. My story was about the Salem Witch Trials but written from the perspective of a man charged to kill witches. I think that Emma could sense the magic radiating from me and after reading my story, she got the courage to ask the question looming in the room.

"Are you…a witch?" she asked timidly.

"Are you?" I retorted.

"It takes one to know one." She grinned. This conversation was the first of real and raw conversations between us.

* * *

Today is the anniversary of my loved ones' death. It is the hardest day of the year to get through. It always causes unpleasant memories and regrets to come flooding back, the waves crashing down on me. Emma suggested that I visit the execution sites and say anything I left unsaid. She volunteered to come with me, and I initially rejected it, believing that this was something I needed to do alone. However, my gut was telling me that I would need her to help me reel from the emotions. She was a witch, although she did not live through it. Emma was not formally taught magic through a coven, because witches were forced into hiding, but she understood the gravity and significance of the day.

I needed to heal from my loss and pain if I ever hoped to move forward and find my remaining loved ones.

I stepped out of the shower, wrapped myself in a towel, and wiped the water vapor from my mirror. I stared at my reflection, searching for the strength to get through the day. I sighed and picked up my hairbrush from the sink and began brushing through my wet hair. I picked out a comb from my medicine cabinet and parted my hair in the middle, whilst I let it air dry. I brushed my teeth and washed my face before turning off the lights and leaving the room. I walked over to my closet and pulled out a black hoodie and blue jeans. It was a dreary day. I needed to feel conformable, for this day would ensure a lot of emotional havoc. I grabbed my makeup bag from the nightstand and walked back into the bathroom. I turned on the light and contemplated whether to apply makeup. I needed a pick me up, something to make me feel more confident. I brushed my eyebrows into place and gelled them down. I put moisturizer on my face, applied lip balm, and then rubbed them together. The day may cause an emotional downpour and I did not want to have to worry about ruining my makeup. I put my lip balm in my pants pocket as I headed back to my room. I unplugged my phone from its charger at my desk and walked over to my bed. I fell backward onto the bed and sighed. I called Emma.

"Hey, Emi. I am ready. Are you guys close?"

"Yeah. You're on speaker."

"Hey, Ryan." Ryan is Emma's twin brother. He has been a great friend to me throughout the years. Our trio has been inseparable in this lifetime.

"Hey, Jo. We should be there in like two minutes. I am turning onto the block now," Ryan asserted.

"OK. I will be out front," I responded. Emma ended the call. I put my phone in my sweatshirt pocket. I stood up and walked over to my closet. I pulled out a pair of white sneakers and bent down to put them on. I stared at my ring as I slipped them on. I missed Charles so much, and this day always brings those feeling bubbling to the surface. I pushed these thoughts away. I needed to remain strong today. I could not let the emotions strike me all at once. I needed to carefully curate my pain, allowing it to slowly burn. If I let all my emotions take over me, I may never be able to pull myself back from the pits of despair. I sprinted down my stairs and exited my house. Ryan and Emma immediately pulled up in Ryan's red sports car. I approached the car and waved at my friends. I pulled on the back door handle and Ryan unlocked the door. I hoped in.

"Trauma-induced road trip time!" Ryan exclaimed. He and Emma look dramatically similar since they are identical twins. However, Ryan does have more masculine features, such as a sharper jawline and wider shoulders. His hair was pulled up into a man bun and he wore a gray T-shirt, a black leather jacket, and black jeans. Emma wore a pink floral dress, brown boots, and a white cardigan. Her hair was slicked back into a high ponytail. The sun was intensely shining in the sky but there was a cool breeze in the air.

"I am kind of hungry. Should we get something to eat before we go?" Ryan said, breaking the thick layer of silence in the car. I think the thought of the Trials, the history of the day, and understanding that if they were born four hundred years earlier, they might have been a part of the statistical casualties.

"Yeah, we might not be up for it later," Ryan responded.

"Yeah. We should get something in you, Joan," Emma said.

"I am game. But let's try not to be here too long. I want to be in and out," I spoke.

"I understand the assignment, girl. I got you," Ryan said.

We stopped for food at a small restaurant with outdoor dining. I was too anxious to eat anything, my stomach was in knots and my heart was racing, I felt as though the whole world was screaming at me and my voice was reduced to a dull whisper.

Ryan was consumed by the menu.

"This place lacks vegan options."

"Stop complaining!" Emma bellowed.

"You brought me here knowing my dietary restrictions. The least you could have done was made sure that there were no animal byproducts here."

"Today is not about you," Emma retorted. Ryan met my eyes and embarrassment flooded through him. I was not paying attention to them. I was thinking of Margaret and how she has been alone for almost four hundred years. Emma grasped my hand and I pulled away, placing my hands underneath the table, on my lap.

"You should eat something Jo," Emma said softly.

"I can't."

"OK, whenever you are ready. Do you want some water?" I nodded, feeling sick, anticipating revisiting the worst day of my life. I gasped and leaned forward nauseated. Emma rubbed my back and Ryan fanned me with the menu.

"You are OK now," Ryan reassured me.

I sat back in my seat. "I'm alright, I think I'm a little under the weather," I groaned. I took a deep inhale, trying to push past the emotions of the day, and put on a brave face. "If you guys can excuse me, I am going to use the laboratory." I rose from my seat and shakily started toward the restaurant door.

Ryan tried to speak softly, obstructing me from hearing him, but his attempt was a failure. I heard every word. "Oh, she's a mess. She is speaking like she is from a different time. She keeps holding in those emotions, it is only a matter of time. That girl is a ticking time bomb."

"This day is always really hard for her. She will be better in no time. Just give her some time to grieve," Emma said.

I cringed and continued to walk inside. I walked through the restaurant, feeling the walk of shame. Everyone was seemingly happy and spending time with family and significant others. I wanted that more than anything in the world. I reached the bathroom. I was hoping for a vacancy, requiring a private moment. A short woman with clear olive skin and a round, protruding midsection was standing in front of a sink vanity applying red lipstick to her lips. She wore a simple cut, off-the-shoulder flowy black dress and jet-black hair was up in a ballerina bun. I walked around her and stood at the sink beside her. I forcefully released a tense breath.

"Rough day?" she asked.

"You can say that." I shrugged, spectating my sickly appearance in the mirror. I turned on the faucet, grabbed a handful of cool water, and splashed my face twice. I shook the water from my hands and pulled a paper towel from the contraption on the wall and dried my face. I could feel this woman staring at me. I turned to meet her gaze.

"Can I help you?" I asked.

"Sorry. It is just that I am a photographer, and you are stunning. Would you mind if I took a photo of you?"

"I don't know…"

"It will only take a second and I can delete it if you do not like it." She interrupted. I turned back to the mirror placing one hand on the bowl of the sink to steady myself and ran my fingers through my hair. I placed my other hand back on the sink.

"Stay just like that." She pulled a black and pink bedazzled camera out of her purse. She held it up a few inches from my face, capturing my profile. She moved it back and studied the image for a few seconds.

"That is gorgeous!" she gushed. She turned the screen around and showed me. I looked lost; a dejected soul hidden behind piercing eyes. My appearance and stance were dreary. The image was slightly out of focus. The photograph was a work of art and symbolic of something I was not wise enough to understand, however, I could tell that it was special.

"It is really good," I said attempting to hide my pain with a cheery disposition. "Thank you," she gushed. "Can I have your email so I can send it to you?"

"Sure." She took out a small notepad and a pen from her purse and handed them to me. I quickly wrote down my email address and handed it back to her. She put them away and placed a hand on her bulging stomach.

"How far along are you?" I asked.

"Twenty-four weeks."

"Do you know the gender yet?"

"The gender reveal is actually in a few weeks. My sister is the only one who knows." She laughed. I joined in feeling awkward.

"That is exciting…Well, nice meeting you…"

"Felicity," she interrupted.

"I am Joan."

"Nice meeting you and thank you for the spontaneous photoshoot. By the way, do you mind if I post this?" She dug in her bag for a moment and pulled out a business card and extended it toward me. I took it and placed it in the back pocket of my jeans. "Sure, go ahead," I said nonchalantly.

"OK. I may just hit you up again to be my model." I laughed and waved goodbye. I left the bathroom and pulled my phone from my jacket pocket. I scrolled through my Twitter feed as I walked hoping to distract myself from what lay ahead for the day. I thought about Ryan and Emma. Hopefully, they already ordered the food, and we could get back on the road soon. I was anxious to get it over with but was in no state to drive myself. As I made my way through the restaurant distracted, my face suddenly slammed into someone. I grabbed my forehead and met this mysterious person's gaze.

"Watch where you're going," I moaned as I dropped my phone.

"Touché," he responded. We bent down simultaneously to retrieve the phone and our hands touched. There was something familiar about him that I could not put my finger on it. I broke eye contact and looked at my hand as I grabbed my phone. The ring I had charmed centuries ago, in hopes of finding Charles was glowing. Could this be it? Had I finally found him?

"Have we met before?" he asked.

I quickly put my phone in my sweatshirt pocket and then covered my ring with my right hand. I stared at him in disbelief. This was the moment I waited for centuries for. "Certainly, feels that way. I am Joan."

"Thomas," he responded.

"Where do I know you from? I swear standing here talking to you, I feel like I have known you my entire life. I feel like you're some I am supposed to remember. Are you a client of mine?"

"It is a long story, but I can…"

"Hey, babe." Felicity stood at Thomas's side. He bent down and kissed her cheek and then returned my gaze still studying me. "I see you met my bathroom model."

"Bathroom model?" he questioned.

"I gave her an impromptu photoshoot in the bathroom." She chuckled.

He turned to her. "You were working, while we're on a date?"

"It is art babe. Inspiration struck." He smiled and shook his head.

"I apologize for my wife." *Wife. He has a wife.* I felt my heart start to die. She laughed and slapped his arm. Felicity dug in her purse and pulled out the camera.

"Look at this beauty." He looked at the image for a second.

"That is brilliant, Ellie." He turned to me. "Do you have modeling experience?" I swallowed hard.

"No…I am a writer."

"Oh, well you definitely have a knack for the modeling industry." He looked down at his watch. "Well, we have to go, but it was nice meeting you…Uh…"

"Joan," I said filling his distorted train of thought.

"Bye Joan." He placed his arm around Felicity, and they retreated from the restaurant. I stoically walked back to the table where my friends were seated. I hid my hands in my pocket, not wanting to discuss my previous conversation. I did not want to digest it, acknowledging my reality, fearing that the pain in my heart would metastasize, leaving me without any legs to stand on. They were eating. Ryan ordered a plate of fries and Emma was eating a turkey sandwich.

"Are you feeling better?" Ryan asked.

"Nope," I said as I shook my head.

"Is there anything we can do?"

"Get me out of here, please," my voice broke and tears streamed down my cheeks. I wiped my face with my sleeve hurriedly and stared at the sky not wanting to gauge their expressions. Emma motioned a waiter over.

"Can I give you a hug?" Ryan asked.

"No, if you hug me, I will cry and I might never be able to stop." I sighed and looked down at my lap. "So just give me a second." I whimpered. "I am not sad. Everything is going to be OK. I am not sad." I mumbled to myself. They exchanged worried glances at each other. A blonde hair blue-eyed waitress came over to the table.

"Is everything OK here?"

"Yeah, we will pay now and take this to go."

"OK, I will be right back," the waitress said. I sat quietly, refusing to speak. After a few minutes of sitting in silence and Emma and Ryan sharing concerned glances, the waitress came back with the bill and to-go boxes. Emma paid the bill and Ryan organized their food in the to-go boxes. We silently walked to the car. I got in the back seat. Emma sat in the passenger seat and Ryan got in on the driver's side. He pulled out of the parking spot and onto the road. We sat in silence for about ten minutes before Ryan broke it.

"How are you doing back there, Jo?"

"I am fine," I said with annoyance.

"You have been a little agitated since you left the bathroom."

"I know. I just...Talk about something else, anything else. Just distract me please."

"Well, you will never believe what happened at work the other day. I walked on set for the independent film I have been working on and my lead actor was like, 'I am not reciting this. The script is trash.' I was like, 'You are acting in an independent film. You have not made a name for yourself and have no influence. Why are you acting all Hollywood?'" He shook his head. "Like not only was he difficult but he also wasn't that great of an actor. He blew my mind. I was so frustrated. I think I might need to recast, but that may set me back a few days on my block schedule, which I don't appreciate!"

"If he is such a nightmare, why did you hire him?" Emma asked.

"I didn't even want to hire him in the first place. Em, the guy I am making the film with, vouched for him. They went to high school together and I guess he owed him a favor. I don't know." He buried his face in his hands and sighed. "He is making my film; my brainchild suck and I can't deal with it anymore. I'm putting my foot down."

"As you should." Emma retorted and snapped in a 'z' formation. Emma and Ryan continued to talk indistinctively. I pulled out my phone and the business card Felicity gave me. I found her social media page. There were a plethora of images of her and Thomas. I found wedding pictures, her photography of both models and landscapes, their pregnancy announcement, candid photos around their home, and cute photos of them on dates or out with friends. The green-eyed monster started to rear its ugly head. I was struck with jealousy. That was meant to be my wedding, my perfect little life with Charles. There was no chance for us now. I cannot be a homewrecker, fracturing his marriage and leaving a child with separated parents. A terrifying thought was now plastered in my mind. What if somehow, he could remember the life, we once had, but still choose his new family over me? My hope was fleeting. The thought of being reunited with him and Maggie was the only thing that anchored me to the earth for so long. That false sense of security was causing my whole world to come crashing down. I felt nauseated by these thoughts.

"Stop the car," I said breathlessly.

"Huh…" Ryan responded.

"Stop the car!" I retched. Ryan pulled over. The car came to a screeching halt, and I leaped out of the car. Emma leaped out of the car behind me and held my hair back. I hunched over onto the sidewalk with one hand on my knee and clenched my stomach with the other as I vomited everything left in my system.

"I think that's it," I groaned. I turned around and climbed back into the car. Emma stared at me for a few seconds, judging if I was truly feeling better or just putting on a brave face. She knew me well enough to decipher the difference. Emma closed my door and then got back to her seat and shut the door behind her.

"OK, this is not just about visiting the site is it," Emma asked in a concerned tone.

"What do you mean? I told you I am a little under the weather."

"Jo, the cat is out of the bag…" She shook her head and I looked out the window. "I saw your ring glow. You met him when you went to the bathroom, didn't you?"

"You don't know what you're talking about?" I said under my breath.

"Come on. Who was he? What was he like? Was it love at first sight?" Ryan said persistently.

"Just stop," I said quietly.

"You have been waiting for him for hundreds of years. And now you find him, and you're doing what? Moping? Why are you here with us? If it were me, I would not be here with you guys," Ryan blurted out.

"I met him, alright. I met him and he is handsome and funny…"

"Oh, I love, love," Ryan blurted out.

"And…married with a child on the way in twenty weeks." Ryan gasped and Emma looked at her feet awkwardly.

"He seems happy and in love and he is getting to start a family. He has the life he wanted. I found him too late…Someone else gave him everything before I could."

"Do you still want to go to the site?"

"Yeah. Now, I have three people to mourn instead of two. More of a reason to go." I started to laugh uncontrollably. Ryan and Emma shared nervous glances.

"You doing OK, sweety?" Emma said sweetly, twisting her body around to see me.

"I can't stop laughing. I spent so many years looking for him and he was busy falling in love with someone else. And he married her…and knocked her up," I continued to cackle.

"Do you want your water, or should we stop and get some air?" Emma asked. Ryan shifted in his seat uncomfortably.

"He told me that he would see me again someday and when our paths are once again intertwined, he has already moved on." My laughing turned into sobs. "He gave up on us and I can't…breathe," I cried. I clutched my chest and began to hyperventilate. Ryan rolled down the windows and I continued to crumble. Emma joined me in the back. She laid me in her lap and stroked my hair.

"Aww, honey this does not mean the end of you guys," Emma reassured.

"This does not necessarily signify the end of your relationship. Life is funny and cruel like that. Maybe in the next life, you will meet again, and he will be single and ready to fall back in love with you."

"He used to have a special place in his heart just for me. As did I. He didn't cheat, he can't remember what we once were. But it hurts a lot. It feels like adultery like he gave up on us. He feels like a traitor and now there is a hole in my heart."

My sobs got quieter, and Ryan began driving again. We sat in silence. Eventually, I drifted off to sleep, reliving my favorite moments with Charles, attempting to push his new persona and life out of my memory. One thing kept me going. He did not remember our love or time together, but he recalled how I made him feel. He felt a connection and only pushed those sentimental, euphoric thoughts of déjà vu away for his wife and mother of his child. A part of him still knew me and wanted me and that revelation gave me hope.

# 12. Take Me Home

It has been eight months of happiness with Nathan. I have moved into his apartment. It is bigger than mine and nicely decorated. The walls are bright blue, and the floors are hardwood. We started off small and worked our way up to higher levels of commitment. At first, I had one draw in his dresser and a toothbrush. Now, we share the place. I got out of the lease from my old place and pay half of the rent on this place. Nathan finished his run in the show and is currently looking for work again. He has been going to audition after audition, hoping to be cast. As I waited for him to come home, I elicited the memory to the forefront of my mind.

* * *

I went to see his last show. Emotions were high, given this was the theatre and show that brought us together. The looming uncertainty of his employment also seemed to stress him out. I could see the tears pouring down the cast's faces as they took their final bows altogether. They received a standing ovation. The show appeared to be superior to the first time I witnesses it. Pride for my boyfriend swelled within me. I wore it like a badge of honor. After the performance, Nathan and I went out to dinner with his cast. They were all so appreciative of their time together and wished us well. They all promised to stay in touch and took commemorative group selfies. When the check came around and everyone was occupied paying their share of the bill, he leaned over to me.

"Move in with me," he whispered. I was astonished, frozen in my seat, staring in my line of sight. I crooked my head and body toward him.

"What did you just say?"

He snickered to himself, "Move in with me."

"You know that is not how we roll in 1600s Massachusetts, Nathan Anthony Roberts." I playfully whacked his arm.

"You're a twenty-first-century woman now." He smirked.

"Do you really want this?" I asked, puzzled.

"Would I have asked twice if I didn't?" he said suavely. "So, what is your answer?"

"I have lived alone for almost four hundred years."

"So, it is about time you have some company, Margaret Evie Baker."

I nodded and smiled wide. "You are scandalous, Nathan Anthony Roberts."

"You know I make your life interesting," he taunted. "Come on. You spend the night all the time, you practically already live there."

"Then why force change?" I tantalized.

"You could have half the dresser instead of a single draw."

"You know in my day you would be required to discuss a dowry with my father."

"Both of our dads are dead. Do I ask him from the great beyond? How is he even supposed to talk back to me?" He chuckled.

"Things were stricter and more routinized back then. Courtship standards are lax now."

"Are you calling me lax for thinking that you're worth more than being purchased from one man to the next? You are not an autographed baseball in a garage sale. You are a priceless person, and I would never think to devalue you in that manner." I shuddered at his remark. I had never viewed that traditional exchange in that manner before. His words were stimulating an internal conflict regarding the traditions that were instilled in me and the discriminatory values behind them.

"OK, you wore me down," my smile intensified. "I will move in with you this week."

He stood up from the table. "She said yes," he exclaimed. The table cheered along with the nearby dining strangers. I looked down at the floor, embarrassed by this outpour of attention. Nathan sat back down in his seat, kissed my hand, and shook it in the air above my head. The room continued to clap for us. I twisted back toward him.

"Are you mad?" he questioned.

"No, it was harmless fun." I giggled. "Was this practice for a real proposal?" I baited.

"Maybe…Maybe not," he provoked. "You will just have to wait and see what the future holds," he teased.

* * *

Nathan came home at seven' o'clock in the evening. I was notified of his presence as the front door slammed. I was sitting in our bedroom down the hall working on lesson plans, answering/sending emails, and creating homework assignments for my students. Without saying anything to me, he walked past the bedroom to the bathroom. I heard the water turn on and I sighed. I rose from my position and closed my laptop. I moved to the kitchen and whipped up mushroom stroganoff in a slow cooker. I heard the water turn off and footsteps approaching the bedroom. I sighed, knowing he was in a mood today. The timer on the slow cooker went off and I opened the cabinet and retrieved two white plates. I opened a drawer and found a serving spoon. I stirred the pot and hummed softly to myself. Nathan came behind me, held my waist, and swayed.

"This smells great, Mags," he whispered. He kissed my cheek.

"Thanks, baby."

He pulled away from me and walked over to the stainless-steel fridge. He opened the fridge door and retrieved a bottle of water. He put his cell phone on the counter and sighed.

"Why are there two plates?" he asked.

I turned to face him. He was wearing a white tank top and yellow basketball shorts. His short damp curls were glistening from the water.

"Are you joking?"

"Nope. I already ate out with Soph."

"That would have been nice information to know," I said stoically.

"Are you upset?"

"Am I upset? You go off to auditions and go out with friends every day. You leave me behind to cook and clean and keep your world from falling apart."

"Oh please! You are kidding me, right!" I rolled my eyes in protest. "I am always taking care of you. I am constantly making sure that your past doesn't consume and destroy you."

"Oh, so now my having to watch my family's execution is a burden to you. Do you just keep me around to stroke your ego, or are you afraid of burning bridges with your freak witch girlfriend? Are you afraid that I might be vengeful if you cut ties, let me down too hard?" my anger overtook me. The lights began to flicker.

"Mags, calm down please," he said softly.

"Did you ever really love me?"

"Look at what you're doing," he said in a concerned tone.

"Is this just a game to you?" The cabinets began to open and slam repeatedly.

"Stop with the magic!" Nathan yelled. I froze, stunned by his aggression. The flickering and the slamming of the cabinets ceased.

"I am sorry. I didn't mean that…" he whispered.

"Tomorrow is the anniversary of their death and I really needed you, OK," I said as tears swelled in my eyes. He walked over to me and embraced me. I buried my face in his chest.

"Why didn't you tell me?"

"Sorry, I can't start crying over this." I buried my face in my hands. He moved closer to me and gently pried my hands from my face. He wiped away my tears and pressed his right hand to my left cheek, smoothing over the skin. I placed my hand over his.

"You are stressed and going through a lot right now." I whimpered.

"Don't apologize for this. You are allowed to be sad, babe."

"I am crying over things that happened almost half a millennium ago."

"And that is perfectly fine. It still hurts. I am not judging you for grieving." He smoothed back my hair. "I love you. You need to be able to talk to me when you are feeling like this. No matter what's going on with us individually, we need to be able to talk to each other."

I looked up at him and nodded. I returned my head to his chest and breathed him in. "Why do you love me?"

"Because you're you. What's not to love?" He said it like it was the most obvious fact in the world. The sky is blue. The sun rises in the east. Nathan Roberts loves Margaret Baker.

"And for the record, I am not scared of you or your powers. You're every comic book nerd's dream." I nodded, not fully believing him. I went off on him and I could sense he was scared. He yawned.

"You should head to bed. I am going to eat and clean up."

"OK babe." He kissed my forehead before pulling away and heading to the bedroom.

I knew that something was wrong with our relationship. I was becoming completely dependent on him. But I didn't care. He was the love of my life. He made every second of every day worth it. Even when I was angry with him or when he said hurtful things, I couldn't bring myself to part ways with him. He was the sun of my life, and I was his.

I placed one of the plates back in the cabinet and dished out a serving for myself. I placed the rest of the food in a Tupperware container and stored it in the fridge. I grabbed a bottle of water from the fridge and sat at the island. I scrolled through social media as I ate. When I finished my food and water, I washed the dishes and the slow cooker and put everything back in their respective places. I used the bathroom and then studied myself in the mirror. Am I genuinely happy with the life I am living? I shook out my frizzy curls. I gathered my hair into my hands and made a bun at the top of my head. I reached into the medicine cabinet and pulled out my facial cleanser and moisturizer. I proceeded to scrub my face with the cleanser and water and then followed it with the moisturizer. I gave my reflection one last glance. I turned off the light and exited the bathroom. I headed into the bedroom, the room was dark, and Nathan was laying on the bed.

"Are you asleep?" I asked quietly.

"Yes." I chuckled softly and climbed into bed next to him.

I laid my hand on his chest and stared into his eyes. He placed his hand on mine and returned my gaze.

"I didn't even ask you, how was your day?" I spoke.

"It was pretty uneventful. I bombed the audition."

"It couldn't have been that bad," I reassured.

"It was atrocious." He laughed.

"Aww. You'll get them next time."

"I sure hope so."

"Hmm…I know so, Nate. I am the witch remember." We chuckled.

"Oh. So, you can predict the future now." Nathan teased.

"Hmm. Let's see. I see fame, bright lights, success, and a beautiful girl standing next to you in your future." He wrapped his arm around my back.

"I see us growing old together. I see a world where no one else exists and I lose myself in you."

"I see myself continuing to feel at home in your arms."

"I think you were made to fit perfectly in my arms." A sentimental grin stretched on his face.

"Speaking of home, let's take a road trip. Show me where you grew up. And while we are there. We can pay respect to your family. It may help you feel better. You have been on edge all week."

I sighed. "I don't know. I have not been back there since it all happened."

"Let me help you." I smiled and rolled over, facing him.

"Do you really think this will help?"

"It won't make the pain completely go away but it may feel good to go to them and have a conversation."

I nodded in agreement. "This is the happiest and healthiest I have ever been, thanks to you. How did I get so lucky?" I kissed his shoulder.

"You aimlessly walked, staring down at your cell phone, in a hustle and bustle city."

"You know, after so many years of isolating myself, I never thought I would get this. I didn't think I could let myself love like this but here we are."

"Oh, I love you so much." He gave me a quick peck.

"Do you really want to go to Salem tomorrow?"

"Mags, take me to meet your parents." He smiled as he swirled his thumb around my fingers and stared up at the ceiling. "I love you and I appreciate you standing by me right now through this. I know I have been in work mode lately and we haven't really had a lot of time together. I just get a little stir crazy during audition season. This business can be so fickle. You can have talent and experience but not have the look the director is looking for and then just like that your cut. It is exhausting, but being on stage, the performance part of it all is exhilarating."

" OK, it's a date." I yawned.

"Road trip," he cheered softly as his eyelids fluttered. I crawled underneath the covers and rolled over. I fell asleep that night dreaming of Joan and my parents. I wondered if they would be proud of me or if they would like Nathan. Would they support my relationship? I knew that our relationship isn't perfect, but I have nothing to compare it to. Nathan is my first love, the apple of my eye. My heart beats for him and only him. I clung to him as hard as I could because he gave my existence meaning and I wouldn't have it any other way.

* * *

*The Next Day*

I woke up the next morning, sick to my stomach. I was excited to spend the day with Nathan, but I was still nervous about the emotions and memories the visit would uncover from my past. I slept restlessly, tossing, and turning throughout the night. I dreamt of life before the Salem Witch Trials. I recalled my old friends and the events that transpired the day prior.

I was walking through the market with my friends, Alice, Henry, Ann, and Jane. Henry and Alice were betrothed, blissfully in love. Jane was the wife of a soldier, who was away in training at the time. Ann and I were among the minority of people our age, unmarried.

"Resurgemus!" Ann shouted. An apple levitated from the display table and floated over to us, landing in the palm of her hand. She shined the apple on her shirt before taking a dainty bite.

"Quit it, Ann." Scuffed Alice.

"I am just trying to have some fun," Ann retorted.

"Go pay for it." Alice sighed. Ann skipped over to the apple stand and handed the worker some coins. Alice was like the mother of the group.

"Why are we here again?" Henry sighed.

"I need fabric to make a dress for the coven meeting tomorrow and Jane needs paint for artwork." Ann returned to the group and wrapped her arms around me.

"How are you doing in your pursuit to find love?" She teased. She removed her arms from around me and walked beside me. We were behind the rest of the group.

"I do not see you with a handsome quick-witted man on your arm."

She sighed. "We need to get out there, find a handsome banker or a perhaps a wealthy musician."

"I do not care about wealth. I want someone who makes me appreciate every sunrise and every sunset, simply because of their presence and tender love and care."

"Hmm. That is a fairytale, Maggie. You know the way of the world. Marriages are political."

I stopped walking and stared at a pale pink fabric.

"That is splendid." I ran over to the table full of fabrics. Jane and Ann followed.

"Aww, look at the way the fabric catches the sunlight. This is the one."

"You are going to look like the fairest witch of all, Margaret," Jane gushed.

"Besides me." Ann inserted. The three of us erupted into laughter.

"Are you wearing a corset, with it?" Jane asked.

"When have you ever seen her in a corset," Ann teased.

"My apologies. I forgot that she was blessed with a tiny waist," Jane teased. Jane created a gust of wind that blew my hair in front of my face.

"Very funny," I said sarcastically and rolled my eyes.

"How did you do that?" Ann asked.

"I have been practicing. I am getting to a place where I no longer need to chant every spell. I can channel the power within me and focus on how I want it to manifest."

"That is incredible," I squealed.

"Please teach that to me," Jane begged.

"An ultimate sorcerer cannot reveal her precious secrets," she teased.

"That is impressive, Jane. You are casting spells like an elder sorcerer," I responded.

"How does it feel to be a prodigy?" Ann mocked.

"It is absolutely glorious," Jane responded.

"How is John?" I asked.

"He is well. He is off living his dream. I get letters from him all the time, he is happy."

"What about you?" I questioned.

"If John is happy, I am happy," she responded meekly. I took her hand and gave it a gentle squeeze.

I shot her a sympathetic glance as I paid for the fabric. We continued walking and eventually caught up to the rest of the group.

"What do you have planned for the meeting?" Henry asked.

"Well, my parents are going to start us off. They will welcome everyone and formally introduce me as the speaker. I am going to go over the traditional spells and then we are going to beautify the neighborhood."

"That sounds lovely, Margaret. Alice and I are overjoyed for you," he responded. Alice shot me a smile, confirming his sentiment. We stopped in front of a table filled with a variety of colorful paints. Jane was an aspiring artist. Her work was deep and abstract. Watching her work, was mesmerizing and inspirational. She had a gift but failed to share it with the world. Only her closest friends were exposed to her art. Seeing it, was like having a front-row seat to the depths of her soul. She retrieved a few cans, and we left the market. That was my last day with my friends. I have no idea what became of them. Did they die in the Salem Witch Trials? Or did they survive and die of old age? I miss our friendship, and the laughs we shared. I miss Jane's artwork and positivity, Ann's sass, Alice's maternal nature, and Henry's compassion. Returning to that place, brought back the light and the dark from my time there. Is going back the right thing to do? Do I need more time away? Am I ready to face the skeletons buried there?

* * *

I was jostled out of my sleep. I turned to see Nathan still deep asleep. I kissed his cheek and got out of bed. I picked up my phone and looked at the time. Intrusive thoughts about Nathan's sincerity in his love for me were percolating through my mind. I quickly pushed them away and walked into the restroom. I hopped into the shower and cleaned myself for the long day ahead. I finished up in the bathroom and headed back into the bedroom and got dressed. I scanned through the closet. I pulled out an emerald-green flowy, ruffle dress and brown ankle boots. Feeling nostalgic, I applied conditioner to my hair and styled it in a half-up half-down style. I put on a pair of diamond stud earrings and applied lip balm to my lips. I stared at my reflection in my wall-length bedroom mirror, and I felt beautiful.

I headed to the kitchen and brewed a pot of coffee for breakfast. While I waited for the coffee, I headed into the living room and made a beeline to the bookshelf. I was searching for a good road trip book. After scanning through multiple titles, I decided on *The Giver.* I placed the novel onto the black couch and walked back into the kitchen. I carried a wooden stool over to the cabinet and climbed on top.

"What are you doing?" Nathan said, laughing. I took out two mugs and climbed down.

"I am very short and needed some assistance reaching the cabinet."

"Aww. I love my shrimpy girlfriend," he teased. He kissed my cheek and walked over to the fridge.

"Ha, ha, very funny." I poured the coffee into the mugs.

"Two sugars?" I asked.

"You know it."

Nathan looked me up and down. "You look beautiful, Margaret Evie Baker."

"You are not too bad yourself. Nathan Anthony Roberts." I smirked.

Nate returned my grin. He opened the fridge door. "Do you want some fruit?"

"No thanks."

"OK, more for me." He pulled out a Tupperware container with fruit salad and placed it on the counter. He walked over to a drawer and pulled out a fork. Nathan started eating the fruit and I grabbed sugar from the cabinet and added it to the coffee.

"So, how are you feeling about going to Massachusetts today?" Nathan asked.

I handed him his coffee. "I am a little anxious about it, but I think it may be good for me." I sighed. "I had a dream last night. Well, it was more like a memory of my friends and me. We were happy and normal, unsuspecting of the horrors that were to come just a day later." I took a sip from my mug. "I don't know what became of them."

"It seems very normal to think of that stuff. Going back is digging up all kinds of emotions and thoughts you probably repressed," he said with his mouth full. Nathan swallowed hard. "We don't have to go if you don't want to."

"No, I want to. I feel like I need to. I don't know how to explain it, but I feel like something is pulling me back there."

"Then let's go on another adventure." He raised his fist in the air in celebration. I chuckled. "Once I am done eating, I will get ready, and we can go."

"Oh my gosh, should I create a road trip playlist?"

"I don't know about that. I think your taste in music is a little questionable."

"How dare you! I am a music connoisseur."

"Are you though?"

"I have lived three-hundred-and-forty-two years. My taste in music is eclectic."

"*I* introduced you to the musical theatre genre."

"Hey, I was alive when Broadway opened in 1735, buddy."

"*Buddy*?" He laughed. "OK, you got me there." He walked over to me, held my waist, and kissed my cheek. "I am going to hop in the shower and get ready for the day."

"Alright, I am going to work on that road trip playlist." I giggled.

"I can't stop you," he teased. He closed the Tupperware container and placed it back in the fridge. He guzzled the rest of the coffee and placed his mug in the sink, before disappearing into the hallway. I finished my drink and washed both mugs, before putting them away in the cupboard. I heard the faucet turn on. The sounds of the water running, and Nathan's angelic singing voice permeated the air. I headed back to the bedroom and grabbed my black bookbag. I carried it with me to the living room and retrieved my book, placing it inside. I then moved to the kitchen and placed two water bottles from the fridge into the bag. I walked back to the bedroom and unplugged my phone. I placed my phone charger in the bag along with my computer and its respective charger. I headed back into the living room and laid on the couch. I pulled out my phone. I scrolled through my playlist, looking for the perfect songs.

"I smell good, I am dressed and I'm ready to vacate the premises." Nathan was dressed in a yellow graphic tee, ripped blue jeans, and white sneakers. I rolled over on my side, facing him, and laughed.

"I think this is the most dressed-up I have ever seen you," I teased.

"Well, first impressions are everything." I smiled, overwhelmed by his compassion. He seemed sincerely enthralled by seeing my hometown and paying respects to my family.

"Alrighty then. Let's get moving!" I said enthusiastically. I stood up and grabbed my bookbag. We walked out of the building and headed to the car, walking side by side. We were a united front, ready to face whatever the world threw at us together. He opened the passenger door for me, and I climbed into

114

the seat. I placed my bag at my feet as Nathan walked around to the driver's side and took his seat.

"Can you put the location in my phone?" He pulled his phone out of his pants pocket and handed it to me. I typed the location into his phone and noted that it would be a three-hour drive.

"Do you want me to drive?" I asked.

"Today is going to be an emotionally draining day for you." He sighed. "You shouldn't have to worry about anything other than your own healing today. Leave the rest to me." He pulled out of his parking spot, and we started on the road.

"Do you want some car tunes?"

"It is your day. Whatever you want." I took out my phone and played our song.

"That is so cheesy. I love it." He laughed.

"This was your move," I teased.

"Well in my defense, I was starstruck by an insanely smart and drop-dead gorgeous woman."

"Well, rumor on the street is the line worked, because the couple is shacked up and madly in love."

"Cheesy joke for the win." We listened to the remainder of the song and the rest of my prepared playlist. After about an hour of driving, Nathan broke the silence.

"I know today is your day and you are supposed to be calling the shots, but I am kind of hungry. Can we get some food?"

"Of course." I giggled. "What are you in the mood for?"

"I wanted some good old fast food, like a juicy burger with a side of fries."

" OK, the next time we near a fast-food restaurant, we are hitting it up."

"Yes!" He cheered.

After about fifteen more minutes of driving, we approached a drive-thru. Nathan ordered a hamburger and fries with a strawberry milkshake. I told him that I didn't want anything. After a while, the smell of his food percolated in the air, and I began to crave it. I ate half of his fries and ended up taking his milkshake. After eating, I pulled my laptop out of my bag and began watching One Tree Hill reruns on my streaming service app.

"How many times have you seen that show?" Nate teased.

"Too many times to count." I chuckled.. Eventually, my eyelids began to feel heavy, and I fell asleep. I dreamt of the morning of the execution, and breakfast with my family except no one died. The house was never broken into, and I never took the elixir. Nathan was not in my life, but I was happy.

When I awoke, we had reached our destination. Nathan was gently rubbing my shoulder as my eyes fluttered open.

"We are here, babe." I stretched and yawned.

"I felt bad waking you up to this, you looked so peaceful," he said dejectedly.

"It's OK. Staring into your eyes is the most settling way to wake," I gushed.

"So, this is where you grew up?"

"Yes, this was my home. Except it is vastly different now." I sighed and pointed at a small house across the way. "That was my home."

He stared at the house, "It was the perfect sized hovel. Not too big to the point where you feel lost, but just the right size for the four of us." I stared off into space visualizing it and getting lost in the pleasant memories.

"It sounds wonderful," Nathan said.

"It really was." I stared down at my feet. "We used to have coven meetings in our lair in the basement."

"What was a coven meeting?"

"The community's witches would beautify the neighborhood, repairing damage left behind by natural disasters or wars. The elder sorcerers would create enchantments that heal the sick. The younger members focused on learning the history of it and perfecting earth magic spells."

"How do you become an elder?"

"The existing elders would induct people as they proved they were ready by completing more complex spells." I sighed, overtaken by the resurfacing memories. I opened the car door and leap out to take a closer look. Nathan swiftly followed me. He seemed nervous; I could tell he was worried about me and how I would handle being back.

I placed my hand in front of my forehead, blocking the sun. "I think they took me half a mile south of here."

"Think?" Nathan questioned.

"They threw a bag over my head halfway through the journey." He placed his hand on my shoulder, "a symbol of his support."

"Let's get back in the car and drive that way," Nate suggested.

116

"It was even hotter that day. I remember my knee giving out as they marched me to my death under the scorching sun. I was reprimanded for my exhaustion. I was manhandled and abused." I swallowed hard, trying to fight the flooding emotions. He placed his hand on my other shoulder and walked me back over to the car. He opened my door and I climbed in. He took his seat and began driving south.

"You tell me when to stop, OK." I nodded.

After about ten minutes of driving, I told Nathan to pull over. I spotted the tree I buried my family's ashes by, the carvings I made that day, were still there, revealing the burial site. I turned to him with tears in my eyes. "Meet my family." We got out of the car, and I led the way to the tree. I knelt in front of it and Nathan retreated a few steps to give me some privacy.

"Hello Mother, Father, Jo. I hope I have been someone you are proud of. I was not living up to the gift you gave me for so long but now I am genuinely happy. I am living this life to the fullest. Not only for you all...but for me too," I said with my voice breaking. "I think I was punishing myself after you died. But I know it wasn't any of our faults. We were victims of troubling circumstances. I am not apologizing for life, but I wish you guys were with me every day. Some days it hurts so bad I want to scream."

Tears streamed down my face, and I wiped them with the back of my hand. "I carry my love for you everywhere I go." I tugged on my pendant. "Mother, I did not retaliate. I did not let them make me into a vicious monster, but I have failed you. Sometimes I wonder if by being me, I was already one all along. I know that is false, just an intrusive thought, and I am working toward pushing that mindset away, but sometimes I cannot help but wonder if we were the monsters. That would make the actions of those men make sense. I have lived on this earth for three-hundred and forty-two years and to this day, it does not make a lick of sense. I was not planning on seeing you all today. I was going to mope around my apartment and pretend like today was not today. But a special someone in my life convinced me to see you. I have someone I want you to meet." I waved over to Nate and once he arrived by my side, I clutched his arm.

"Nathan, this is my family." I looked at him and then directed my attention back to the tree.

He cleared his throat. "It is nice to meet you...I am Nathan Roberts. Margaret has told me a lot about you. I just wanted to thank you for creating her and molding her into the person she is today. I watch her battle her demons every day because of the courage, compassion, and determination you instilled in her. She single-handedly is unlearning the hatred those people placed in her heart when they took you away from her. I am so proud to call her my girlfriend, the love of my life." He began tearing up. "Thank you for bringing her to me. I promise to do right by her and to love her until my last dying breath."

I turned to him with tears swelling in my eyes and said, "Till the end of time."

"I will love you until the oceans are dust, Margaret Evie Baker," he responded. He leaned in toward me and I stopped him by putting my hand on his chest.

"No in front of Mother and Father," I whispered.

"I think they have been watching over you all along," he whispered. Our lips touched and sparks flew. I pulled away from him and wiped my tears with the back of my hand.

"I am sorry, I am snotting all over you." I snorted.

"It is OK. I am blubbering like a baby too." I wrapped my arms around his neck and pulled him into my embrace. He placed his hands around my waist, and we stood there, frozen in the moment.

"Do you want to go back?" he asked.

"I would like that." We held hands and headed to the car. He held the door open for me once again and we both took our seats. We drove back to the house.

"Can we stop here for a moment? I just want to say goodbye," I said softly.

"Of course, babe." He parked across the street from the house. We got out of the car and approached the home. Two women and a man stood in front of the house.

"Hello. Are you the homeowner?"

"No, I used to live here once upon a time," the tall red-haired woman responded.

"Me too," I responded. Was it a coincidence that she chooses to visit on this day? Something about her demeanor, the way she carried herself seemed familiar. I stared at her intently, studying her.

"Everything OK, Margaret?" Nathan asked. The group all sharply turned to me, and their eyes grew wide.

The woman I had been staring at gasped and beamed at me. "Is your name Margaret baker?"

"How do you know my name?" I retreated closer to Nathan.

"I am your sister, Joan." I looked at her suspiciously.

"My sister died." She shook her head.

"No, I drank it before you did. I lived. I have been looking for you for three-hundred and twenty-three years." She ran toward me and brought me into her embrace.

"Joan." I whimpered.

"It is me," she cried. She smoothed my hair, looked into my eyes, and pulled me back into her embrace.

# 13. Where the Lost Things Go

*Joan's Point of View*

I entered my old address into the GPS of Ryan's phone. After about half an hour of driving around, we arrived at the location of my childhood home. Ryan found a parking spot on the block. A new house was built over the empty lot. There were more houses, and they were of a more modern stature. Everything was different but muscle memory of how this place made me feel lingered. I could feel the happiness, nostalgia, and devastation all at once. Memories, both good and bad came rushing back. I stared out the window amazed by how this place still had a tight hold on me almost four hundred years later. My phone buzzed and I pulled it out. I received an email notification. It was an address I didn't recognize and there was no subject line. Curious about this mysterious message, I opened the email. It read:

*Hi,*

*My name is Thomas. We spoke earlier in the restaurant. My wife gave you an impromptu photo shoot in the bathroom. I hope I am not bothering you. I know why your face is so familiar. You're the woman I see in my dreams. I get frequent visions of you and me. It is like another time; we are in ancient outfits at a stable. Seeing you today felt like I have been around you before. I promise I am not crazy. Do you have these too?*

*Best regards,*

*Thomas Allen.*

I smiled. A semblance of our love lived within him. We had unfinished business with another life, so the universe must be pushing us together in this one.

"Do you want to get out and walk from here or should we keep driving around?" Emma drew me away from my thoughts.

"Let's walk from here," I said, still looking at the house. I removed my seat belt and opened the door hastily. I stood there staring in awe, marveling how time carried on and I was still standing in the same place, harboring the same dilemmas. I felt as though everything and everyone was evolving, leaving me to dwell on the past.

I turned north. "I think they took me this way…I will recognize the area when I see it." Of course, I would the image is plaster in my nightmares, the cause of my suffering. It is the place I identify as the location where my life took a turn for the worse. Before we could turn to push on, a woman interrupted us.

"Hello. Are you the homeowner?" a timid voice said.

"No, I used to live here once upon a time."

"Me too," I responded. I did not think much of this response. I am sure many people occupied this lot in the past three-hundred and twenty-three years.

"Everything OK, Margaret?" a man beside her asked. Ryan, Emma, and I all sharply turned to me, and our eyes grew wide in disbelief.

I beamed at her, suspending my disbelief, "Is your name Margaret Baker?"

"How do you know my name?" she asked petrified and retreated closer to her male companion.

"I am your sister, Joan." She looked pensive. I could sense that she didn't believe me.

"My sister died," she retorted. I shook my head.

"No, I drank it before you did. I lived. I have been looking for you for three-hundred and twenty-three years." I ran toward her relieved to finally be in each other's presence. I wrapped my arms around her and held on for dear life, fearing losing her again.

"Joan." She whimpered.

"It is me," I cried. I brushed her hair away from her face with the palm of my hand, looked into her eyes, and then gathered her petite body back into my arms.

"I love you, little sister." I whimpered.

"I love you," She cried out.

I stood up tall and wiped away my tears. "Who is this gentleman accompanying you?"

"Oh, this is my boyfriend, Nathan. Nathan, this is Joan." I extended my hand toward him, and he grasped it and gave a nervously vigorous handshake.

"Nice to meet you," I charmed.

"Likewise, Margaret speaks fondly of you."

"She better," I joked. Margaret looked down at my left-hand ring finger.

"Interesting jewelry." She snickered and then paused. "Oh my gosh! Are you married? I missed my chance to be your bridesmaid. I was supposed to make you the most stunning dress. What did you even wear, some cheaply made store-bought one?" She said in one breath.

Emma grabbed Ryan's arm and waved over to Nathan. "We are going to give you too some space." I nodded at them, and they began to walk away. Nathan followed their lead.

I looked down at my hand. "This was from Charles."

"Did you find him after? Did you guys get married?" She gasped. "Oh, you had to watch him die of old age while you lived on."

"No, he watched me die, during the Trials. They killed him after, they killed me."

She took my hand. "I am so sorry Jo."

"It is alright. You did not know."

"I found his reincarnation today."

"How is that possible?"

"We had unfinished business. I think of it as a higher power giving us another chance."

"So, where is he now?"

"He is married." Maggie gasped.

"What are you going to do?"

"The only thing I can do is move on."

"It is a little ironic that I am the one in a relationship now." She chuckled awkwardly. "Nathan is perfect. He is a musician; he even wrote me a song. I think we are soulmates." I nodded my head.

"That is great. I am really happy for you." I cleared my throat. "Would you excuse me for a moment?"

"Sure. But hurry, back. We have a lot to catch up on."

I swiftly headed in the direction of our departing friend group. How could she be so tone-deaf? I was heartbroken and she was selfish, only concerned with her happiness. Happiness that belonged to me once upon a time.

Lost in my thoughts, I collided with Nathan's back. He turned around startled. His expression softened when my face came into focus.

"Oh, umm…Hi Joan." He paused; silence permeated the air between us. Emma and Ryan continued to walk unaware that we had stopped. "You and Margaret got a tough break. You both deserve the world."

"So, you and Margaret are serious, huh."

"Think of it like this, the best part of my day is waking up next to her and falling asleep beside her. She loves me, for the good, bad, and plain ugly. I see that you're a protective sister, but I want you to know that I have nothing but good intentions."

"You know, Margaret doesn't love you. She loves the idea of you. She loves love." He contorted his face in confusion.

"She is a naïve little girl who romanticizes what I had at her age. She wants the whole nine. A man who can provide for her and take care of her. She wants to clean and cook and have your babies. She has no idea what real love is. Love is a drug and once you are dependent on it, it chews you up and spits you out."

"Are you alright?"

"I am better than alright." He scratched his head confused by my advances.

"I am finally seeing what I have been blind to for all these years. I can't rely on a man to make everything OK. I must steer my own fate. Go after what I want." Nathan shifted uncomfortably and I took a step toward him. "Maggie desires a traditional little family. You're young, you have your whole life in front of you. You don't want that. Dodge the bullet…Have fun with me." I smirked and gently placed my hand on his bicep.

"You've lost your mind…"

I placed my pointer finger over his lip and leaned in. "You're attracted to me. Don't fight it," I whispered. I wrapped my arms around his neck and kissed him. I was angry, tired of being a punching bag for the world's amusement. I lost everything and when I found some resemblance to my former life, they both moved on, happy without me, while I festered in misery. They were my driving force throughout my existence, and without them, I felt weightless, like I could float away to a meaningless spec on the earth. He pulled away.

"What are you doing? I am your sister's boyfriend! I love Margaret!" he exclaimed.

"Please," I said breathlessly. "I need this."

"I am sorry, but I am not the person you're looking for," he groaned.

He headed back to Maggie, and I stood there in disbelief, ashamed of myself. I don't know what came over me. On this day, seeing Maggie perfectly adjusted and experiencing the love I once had and acknowledging that my love story with Charles had overturned me into a person I was not proud of. I was in pain and Nathan was just there. I wanted revenge. I wanted others to hurt the way I did, and the regrets flooded in almost immediately. I didn't realize I wanted Charles and when I finally found him, it was too late. I was jealous and irate and plastic toward the people around me. So much of my identity in the last four centuries was formed around finding them and they no longer needed me. I became useless, a seemingly waste of space, in the blink of an eye.

* * *

*Margaret's Point of View*

I took a bottle of water out of my bag and savored a large sip. Nathan walked back over to me. His face was contorted, and his demeanor gave away his nervousness. I laughed. "Does my sister make you nervous?" He opened his mouth to speak, and I interrupted him. "That is so cute." I kissed his cheek, "She is a little protective, but you have nothing to worry about. I love you and she said that she is happy for us." I beamed.

"That is great, babe," he responded bashfully.

"Are you ready to go?" he asked.

"Oh, we should ask Joan to come back with us. We have so much sister bonding time to catch up on."

"We can't ask her to uproot her life on such short notice, babe."

"Nate, I thought she was dead. We have not seen each other in almost four hundred years."

"Fine. Today is your day after all. Go for it."

I studied him, concerned. I placed my hand on his cheek and then moved to his forehead. He looked pale and drained like something sucked the life right out of him. "Are you feeling, OK?" I asked.

"Yes, I think I am just a little dehydrated." I opened my bookbag and handed him a water bottle.

"I am always prepared."

"My responsible queen," he said, before kissing my forehead. I watched him twist open the bottle and guzzle the water until the bottle was empty.

"That was oddly satisfying," I remarked.

He smiled. "Alright, let's head back because it is going to take us a few hours to get home. It is getting late, and I don't know these roads." We scurried over to Joan and her friends.

"I'm sorry. I was so caught up in the family reunion, I totally forgot to introduce myself. I'm Margaret."

"I'm Emma."

"Ryan."

"Good to meet you guys. Thanks for taking great care of my sister." They nodded and I transferred my gaze to Joan.

"Hey, do you want to come back with us?"

"I don't know about that Maggie."

"Please, just for the weekend. Come on. We have been apart for so long." She caved under my persistence.

"Fine, I would love to spend the weekend with you."

"This is going to be so great. We can do face masks, paint each other's nails and watch sappy romantic comedies."

"The sleepover to end all sleepovers." She chuckled.

Joan hugged Emma and Ryan and thanked them for accompanying her.

When she returned to my side, I blurted out.

"Today went the best it could have gone." She nodded in agreement. We walked to Nathan's car in exasperating silence. He pulled his key chain out of his pants pocket and unlocked the car door. As usual, Nathan opened my car door, and I took my seat on the passenger's side. Before Nathan could perform the same chivalrous gesture to Joan, she opened the door and swiftly took her seat, and closed the door. Joan is as self-reliant and rebellious as I remember. She is a firecracker, a force to be reckoned with. I cannot wait to hear the tremendous stories and circumstances of her extended life. Nathan took his seat, closed his door, and placed our address in his GPS.

"So, how far away did you move?" Joan piped up.

"Three hours from here. I am a New Yorker now," I responded.

"Do you like it there?"

"It is vibrant and lively. It has become home."

"What do you do?"

"I am a teacher. I teach kindergarten at a Catholic School in the city."

"Are you content with teaching? You must have tried out several professions over the years."

"I have. I have pursued being a nurse, and a nanny. I just enjoy working with children. I am some of their first experience with school. I get to not only mold their minds but their relationship with learning. It's so rewarding." Nathan pulled out of the spot and started on the main road. He seemed tensed and uncomfortable. I felt compelled to ask him about it but did not want to make Joan feel uncomfortable on the long car ride with us.

"That sounds lovely, Maggie."

"What do you do?"

"I am a writer."

"Really? Why haven't I come across your name? I have an extensive book collection, you know." I chuckled.

"I write under pseudonyms. It allows me to write in each lifetime without being discovered."

"You are going to have to look through my book collection and tell me which of my favorites are actually written by you." I smirked.

"Sounds like a plan, little sister." Her voice died out and re-emerged. "Do you still practice magic?" she asked.

"What would be the point?"

She pinched her face in anger. "To keep a family tradition, a part of who we are alive."

"Don't get mad. It is not that serious."

"Maggie, they killed us for being witches. By stopping your training, you let them win. Is it because your new bae is magicless?" Nathan gave me a glance with his guilty, bright brown eyes.

I retaliated, offended by her harsh words. "I stopped because I wanted to. You let them win by giving up on Charles and festering in your anger." Nathan shifted uncomfortably in his seat.

"I did not give up on Charles. He is a different person now. He moved on," she sneered.

"You let him go," I jeered.

Nathan took his eyes off the road for a second, turning to me.

"Ease up on her," he whispered.

"So, you are the expert on relationships now? Margaret, you were there that day, you experienced it with me. Our world was set ablaze, and you are complaining about the inconvenience of the resulting ashes."

"That is not what I am saying, Jo. I just want you to be happy."

"Not everyone's happy ending revolves around a man," she inserted.

I rolled my eyes. "You said that before."

"And I exchanged vows with him on our deathbeds."

"What are you talking about?"

"Oh, you have been so occupied with your relationship. You did not even try to get the details of what happened before you placed judgment. He proposed to me while we were cuffed to the stake, scared out of our minds, facing our early demise. We exchanged vows and then my skin was set ablaze."

"You can't use that as an excuse to avoid falling in love."

"I don't want to be in love!" Joan exclaimed.

"Everyone wants love."

"You are a hopeless romantic. I am happy right where I am. Just let me be."

"You and Charles were cheated out of your lives together. That is an even bigger incentive to fight for him."

"That only happens in the movies, Maggie."

"No, you just have to be willing to gamble with your heart, opening yourself to the possibility of rejuvenated romance or rejection."

"You don't understand."

"You are being childish." I rolled my eyes and sighed in annoyance.

"I am childish. You are trying to recreate some romantic fantasy cinematic ending for me and Charles. This is real life. My life. This is not a movie. He is happy without me."

Nathan turned to me again. "I think you should stop," he whispered. I shook my head in defiance.

"What happened when you met him today?"

"It is none of your business."

"I am your sister. We used to talk about everything."

"That was over three hundred years ago Margaret." She sighed. "We have not been sisters to each other in an exceedingly long time. I love you and I will always love you. But I am not ready to talk about this and I need you to respect that," she said calmly.

"You're avoiding the question."

"Did you even hear what I just said?" She paused for a moment. "This was a mistake. Nathaniel, stop the car."

"Nathan, keep driving. We need to talk about this."

"No, we don't. We are strangers to each other. I don't understand how you can be so similar and yet so different."

"How can you be so dense. We have lived how many lifetimes. You should know that life is pointless without someone to share it with. Nate has given my life meaning and made me appreciate every single day."

"That is amazing, Maggie. You know what? That moving story made me a changed woman. I am going to run to Thomas and be America's favorite homewrecker," Joan said sarcastically.

"You are mocking me."

"You are so tone-deaf. It is unbelievable. Can you remember a time before Nathan? A time when our past haunted you. You seem so well adjusted. You act as if this day doesn't tear you up inside, but I know the truth. I was there. I can see it in you. You have survivor's guilt and seeing me alive, alleviated some of that guilt but I know it still exists."

"Are you done chastising me?"

"Are you done being a naïve child? For goodness's sake, act like an adult."

"Who hurt you? Why are you so mean?" I asked turning to meet her gaze. She stared directly into my eyes.

"This day cut me deep and you are pouring salt in my wounds."

"It was traumatic for me too…"

"How do you do that? You shift the conversation and make everything about you. You are always either the victim or the pinnacle example of how others should model their behavior in your narcissistic head."

"Your anger has maddened you. You are sick."

"You're a lovesick puppy dog, begging at the feet of someone who will never really love you."

I balled my fist in anger. "I feel sorry for you."

"I feel sorry for you too. Ask your precious Nathan what happened between us?"

I turned to him with tears swelling in my eyes. "What is she talking about?"

He stayed focusing on the road. "How about we change the subject?"

I raised my voice. "What is she talking about?"

"It is nothing," he said calmly.

"What is nothing?" I persisted. He shook his head in protest. "Tell me," I shouted. Dreaded silence filled the room as tears streamed down my warm flushed cheeks.

He sighed. "We kissed." I gasped. "But it was not romantic. It was merely platonic...I love."

"Stop talking!" I yelled. I sighed. "My own sister. I welcomed you back into my life and in like twenty minutes you are uprooting the foundation I built, taking it for yourself. He is my boyfriend, the love of my life. I told you how much he means to me, and you coveted him for yourself."

"He isn't a prized horse, you can claim as your own."

"Shut up!" I aggressively remarked. "I want you out of my life. You were right earlier. You are broken. You let those men break you that day. You are an angry, miserable shell of the woman and sister you use to be."

I stared at the roof, fighting back the flood of tears. "Nathan, turn this car around. Call your friends and arrange for them to pick you up."

"That is a little dramatic. Let's go home and talk this out, babe," Nathan remarked.

"Don't call me babe! You lost that privilege went you locked lips with my sister!"

"First of all, she kissed me, and I immediately ushered her away."

"Then why didn't you tell me. I should have heard it from you," I sobbed.

"Because today is already a loaded day for you. I was going to tell you when the time was right." He scratched his head. "Joan was in the wrong, but do not assign her all blame. She is traumatized just as much as you are. She made a mistake."

"Oh, so now you are defending her. You want her to be your girlfriend now?"

"That is not what I said. You are being irrational."

"I should have known you were too good to be true. How could I be so stupid?"

"Mags, I am so sorry. I did not mean for this to happen."

"You cheated on me with my sister. Did you know her before you met me?"

"No," Joan chimed in.

"Do not talk to me!" I yelled. "I do not want to hear it from you. You have done enough," I exclaimed.

"You are acting like a child," Joan responded.

"You are a little too old to be embodying the mean girl cheerleader who steals everyone's boyfriends," I remarked. "How are you so stoic right now. You can't get Charles, so you try to steal my happiness for yourself. Do you realize how hard it was for me to allow myself to feel content with life? How dare you take this from me?"

"It was never my intent to hurt you."

"But you did." I sighed. "The damage has been done."

"I messed up, OK," she whimpered.

I banged my fist on the glove compartment twice, festering in my frustration. "You messed up? Is that intended to make everything OK? Coloring outside of the lines is messing up. What you did is burning bridges." I rested my hand on the arm rest, attempting to steady my anger-stricken, trembling body. Nathan removed a hand from the wheel and placed it on top of my hand. I snatched my hand away from his and he moved his hand back to the wheel.

"Did you even mean the things you said at the grave today?"

"Of course."

"Not of course! Your love isn't definite if you are kissing other women. I trusted you. Do you understand how big of a deal that is? I dusted off my rusty heart to let you in. I shared my secrets, my desires. I know that I am not your first, but you are, or at least you used to be, my everything."

Nathan sighed. "We should continue this conversation later, Margaret." He turned on the radio and a dance song permeated the air.

I pulled out my phone and began angrily typing. "What are you doing?" Nathan asked.

"I am researching hotels near your apartment. Figured you and my sister could use some space."

"I know you are rightfully mad at me right now. But despite what you may think, I love you and I have since the first day I met you. And I plan to until the oceans are dust." We sat there in silence. I refused to acknowledge the absurdity I felt regarding his statement. He fixed his mouth to speak again and then decided against it. My heart hung heavy with the loss of my admiration for the two people I love most in this world. I felt as though my head would explode with the nightmare-filled fantasies of Nathan and Joan being together. I was beyond hurt and vocalizing my newfound disdain for them did little to satisfy me. Joan indistinctively yelled something. I was annoyed by her voice, cringing in my seat. Didn't she understand that she was in the wrong and pestering me with making her presence known? We were in a moving vehicle, with no way to escape each other. Could she give me the decency to disappear again?

"Watch out!" Joan cried out. The car swerved, sharply changing lanes at high speed. I heard a loud bang as we collided with another vehicle. The car jerked and the force of the collision caused me to bang my head on the dashboard. The impact caused my world to go black. Maybe I should have worn my seat belt. I was full of excitement and anticipation upon my initial seating in the car. And once Nathan and Joan's betrayal was revealed, I was sucked into the madness of deceit and mistrust. I dreamt of my sister, her words like a gun firing at me. I pictured her tall slender build snuggling up to Nathan, her fingers combing through his dark curly hair. Her lips draped over his and a devilish smile stretched across her face. This was not a dream but a hellish nightmare and, in every frame, Nathan seemed to be content, opposing her affections. My sister, a cunning, treacherous temptress, gunning for everything I hold dear. What's next? My job? Why did she revel in my misery? What did I do to her? What did I do to deserve the rug pulled from underneath me? I was finally content, at peace, no longer harboring this survivor's guilt. She ruined everything in the few minutes she entered my life and for that, I held her in contempt and regarded her with unyielding repugnance. A memory resurfaced of the girl, the best friend I use to hold in such high esteem.

* * *

Joan had talked me into horseback riding with her and Charles. I was excited to spend time with the man who held her infatuation but was revolted by the idea of being in a mucky stable with malodourous animals. It was unladylike, unrefined, and repulsive, but Joan asked me to accompany her, so I did as she requested. We walked together to the stables. Joan made me wear the appropriate riding garments and forced me to tie my hair up. I thought the large clothing that I put on made me look like a man and was ashamed to be seen in public. I wore one of Father's large cavalier hats to shield people from

131

seeing my humiliating attire. Joan thought my sheepish behavior was ridiculous but did not quarrel with me about it. I could tell that she was excited to see Charles, the center of her world, and ignored her displeasure with me. We got to the stable in a short amount of time. Joan pulled me along, every step of the way. Joan danced into the stable and I dragged behind her, reluctant to go inside. Charles stood inside brushing a large chestnut horse.

Joan pranced over to him and gave him a peck on the cheek. "I brought Maggie with me today. She has never ridden a horse," she said softly. I awkwardly waved at Charles, wanting to leave the stable and run home.

Charles walked toward me and pulled me into his embrace. "Nice to see you again." I was taken back by his outpour of affection.

"The pleasure is all mine."

He pointed to the bay brown horse in the far corner. "That one is yours for the afternoon."

I gave him a weak smile and timidly approached the horse. I stood before it and hesitantly reached up to pet its nose.

"You need not worry, Margaret. She is gentle. She will not cause you harm." I petted the animal, and she bowed her head at my touch. She let out a loud nay and I stumbled backward.

"You are fine, little sister. Horses are supposed to make noise," Joan chimed in. She let out a loud chuckle, finding my growing fear comical. She and Charles took hold of the reins of the respective horses and led them onto the trail. I followed their lead, walking behind, terrified of the creature behind me. Joan walked with a brown horse and seemed to be comfortable. Did she not smell the putrid musk in the air? How could anyone find this enjoyable? They stopped and climbed onto the backs of their horses. I stopped in my tracks and struggled to mount on my horse's back.

"Do you need help," Charles asked.

"No, I almost got it." I was stubborn and mortified. After a few more tries, I successfully mounted the horse and sat side-saddle.

"Come on, Maggie. Do not be such a priss," Joan blurted.

"I will not ride like a man, Sister. Good thing you already have a dedicated suitor."

"Let loose, Maggie," she replied. I rolled my eyes in protest, refusing to take her advice. I was still waiting to attract a suitor and feared an eligible bachelor may see me being anything less than ladylike. I kept my position as we moved along the trail. I found the ride to be boring and uneventful. Joan really did meet her match if they engaged in this activity willingly.

We carried on like this for what seemed like an eternity. I was beyond bored. I began counting trees along the path and identifying images the clouds made in the sky. My horse was spooked by something. The horse whined and pranced frantically before throwing me off and running away. I laid injured, face down in the dirt. Joan and Charles dismounted from their horses and fled to my side. Joan tore the sleeve from her shirt and wrapped it around the deep wound on my knee. I felt Charles scoop me into his arms.

"Give her to me," demanded Joan.

"I am going to carry her back to your home."

"Charles, do you really want to fight me on this?" Her voice was rough and tinged with the strength of her resolve. Her determination was always the thing I admired most about her. Charles let out a long sigh and then placed me in her arms.

"That is what I thought," Joan said smugly. She carried me home and stayed by my side as our parents examined me. She watched over me as the wound healed. My sister was my fiercest protector. So, her betrayal today baffled me and seared hatred and bewilderment into the depths of my heart.

* * *

I was so captivated by him that I did not realize that I was a captive in our relationship, a locked gate embedded over my heart, and Nathan was the gatekeeper possessing the only key. My friends were his and I lived in his home. I thought our love was a bouquet, blooming with perfect red roses, but I ignored the prickly thorns within, ignoring the blood-soaked stain of deceit, mistaking them for blossoming flowers that I hoped, in time we could foster. I'd hope that we can grow a grandiose garden from the seeds of love we planted inside each other. But the soil is barren and rocky unyielding to my desires.

Isn't it funny how the world works? The sister you once admired, adored, and mourned betrays you, making your admiration a distant memory. The guy who turned your world deceives you. The world you once knew is spinning off its axis. Unfortunately, this is average, a typical day in life. Betray is an old bitter song that rings in the ears of many. Today, once again, the retched song rang clear amongst the sweet, melody of young love. It's the way the world works and predates my existence. Betrayal is a story that dates to Genesis, the beginning of life. I should not be surprised; I closed my heart off from love for a reason. I have witnessed empires rise and fall, and genuine and malicious rulers succumb to deceit and betrayal. The good, the bad, and the moments of indifference are chapters in everyone's tale, and they come in waves. Could this be my final chapter in this life? Will this lethal motif be my undoing?

Nothing in this crude, treacherous world holds permanence. One day you are floating above sea level, drifting as a gentle wave lifts you and carries you away to an island of bliss. And the next the tide pulls you under and the ocean swallows you whole. Hopefully, someday soon, the tides will turn, and I will re-emerge jovial at last.

# 14. Rude Awakening

*Joan's Point of View*

I watched, horrified and ironically powerless as the vehicle collided with another and Margaret's head slammed against the dashboard. Nathan sat there, eyes wide, stuck in a state of complete and utter shock. I pulled my phone from my sweatshirt pocket and called an ambulance. I fought the instinct to drag Margaret from the vehicle, fearing I would worsen any injuries she sustained in the collision. The other car had crashed into the car on Nathan's side. Causing the car to swerve onto the side of the road. The airbags went off in both cars and the other driver, a seemingly middle-aged white male, was unconscious. I swallowed hard as the operator intercepted the call.

"911, what's your emergency?" a female operator's voice said.

"My sister, her boyfriend and I just got in a car accident. The car hit the driver's side of the car. I am in the back, so I was shaken but not injured," I said stoically. "We are on the I-95 south, close to the Colden exit."

"OK, help is on the way. Is everyone breathing? Can you feel their pulse?" I unbuckled my seatbelt and crawled onto the armrest. Hunched over and contorted to fit the small space, I placed two fingers on Margaret's neck. I could feel the blood rushing, pulsating under the skin.

"I can feel it!" I exclaimed, relieved.

"OK, how about the other passenger?" I turned toward Nathan awkwardly, still uncomfortable in the tight space. I picked up a limp hand from the steering wheel and placed two fingers on the inside of his wrist. Again, I felt the blood rushing in the arteries under the thin skin.

"His heart is beating. There is still blood flow," I remarked. I placed his hand back on the steering wheel.

"OK, do you have eyes on the driver?" the lady asked.

"He is unconscious. The airbags went off."

"Alright, stay put and remain calm. The ambulance should be there any second," the lady reassured.

I returned to the back seat and lay across it with the phone on my chest. I was relieved that help was coming and that my sister and Nathaniel are still alive but who knows what internal damage the crash could have inflicted. The thought of it terrified me. Nathan's eyes were now open, but he remained motionless, in shock. I silently debated whether I should shake him back to reality or let the medical professionals handle it. I took a deep breath and sat up.

"Nathaniel, can you hear me?" I called out. There was no response. I scooted forward and laid a hand on his shoulder. I began to gently tap him.

"She is going to be OK. This isn't your fault, Nathaniel. " I looked at the mirror, his eyes were filling with tears, and he began to shake his head.

"She's unconscious but she is breathing. That is good, OK. We are all going to be fine. Help is coming."

"She's OK?" he tried to turn toward her, and I gripped his shoulders stopping him. "You are in shock, adrenaline is coursing through you, and you may not be able to feel the full extent of your injuries. You need to stay put."

"How did this happen?" Nathan asked. "We were arguing and then a car came out of nowhere and ran us off the road." He sighed.

"Everything will be fine. We need to remain positive and stay calm." I did not believe the words pouring out of my mouth. This situation was not ideal, and Margaret was still out. If she died, she would awake in another form, and due to our last conversation, she would not be looking to find me or Nathan. She would be lost to us both for the foreseeable future. As annoyed as I was with her, I was not prepared to lose her once again. I heard the sound of the sirens and sighed in relief. We were all quickly assessed and loaded into the back of the ambulances. I was deemed healthy and rode with Maggie refusing to leave her side. Nathaniel rode in the ambulance ahead of us, causing him to reach the hospital first. He had lacerations on his head and required a full neurological workup and possible MRI imaging. I thought of my little sister. The impact on her head may have caused a brain bleed, which would explain her decreased level of consciousness and the EKG abnormalities on the monitors. She may also have internal bleeding in the abdomen from her blow against the dashboard. She was obviously tired, and her skin had lost some color. My heart ached for her; the remorse consumed me. My sister, my first friend, could die hating me.

They brought us to a nearby hospital and set us up in the busy emergency room. Maggie was swiftly assessed and then taken for a full-body scan. I could not bear the sight of her empty room and moved to the nurse's station. A young man sat behind the desk, occupied by the computer in front of him.

"Excuse me, I was wondering if I can see my friend, Nathan Roberts? Can you direct me to his bed?"

"What is your relationship with the patient?"

"I am his significant other." I lied through my teeth. Because we are not family, they cannot give personal information away, but they may be more inclined to if I tell them that we have a relationship.

He looked back down at his computer and began to type. "He is in bed number 7."

I smiled wide and nodded. "Thank you." I walked over to his bed. He was dressed in his street clothes, and his head was bandaged. I walked over to his bed and stood over his slouched form.

"How is she?" he asked.

"She's in imaging right now." He swiped his hands over his face and exhaled loudly.

"I need to see her when she gets out," he said firmly.

"I know," I reassured.

"I need to tell her I am sorry and…" His voice began to break. I placed my hand on his shoulder, intending to comfort him.

"No, stop!" he exclaimed. "We can't do this."

"You are clearly distressed, and I am just trying to be a compassionate human being," I said with agitation behind my words.

"Joan, I just don't need this from you right now," he said as he leaped to his feet, pushed the curtain aside, and marched out of the room.

I ran after him and followed him to the cafeteria. He sat at a table by himself. I took a seat across from him.

"She isn't going to be in her room for a while," he blurted. I nodded.

"Do you want something to eat?"

"I can't eat until I know she is OK." He shook his head in protest.

"Don't beat yourself up over it. I was a nurse a century ago. Medical practices have changed since I practiced but I think she will be OK." I lied through my teeth, withholding my feelings and opinions on Margaret's well-being in a mediocre attempt to soothe his guilt and my own. But I knew that Margaret would need more than imaging before she could go home. He nodded, convinced by my lie.

"Now, how do you take your coffee?" I rose from my seat and shot him a reassuring grin.

"Two sugars, no milk."

"One coffee with two sugars coming up." I chuckled and walked over to the machine, carefully pouring one cup of pure black coffee with added sugar and one diluted with milk.

I thought of Margaret. I recalled watching her lying on that hospital bed limp and unconscious. I remembered her petite, fragile frame and how mangled she could be internal. I was growing anxious and impatient, needing to see her safe. I may need to whip out a healing spell. How could I successfully administer this without the unsuspecting mortals seeing my witchery? I also required ingredients to anchor the spell to Margaret. I needed to devise a plan, giving me ample time alone with her. I would need about five minutes to prepare the ingredients and about three minutes to enact the spell if I perform everything perfectly. Everything should work out well. I enacted this ritual frequently back in my time and when I worked as a nurse in the mid-1900s. I returned to the table and handed Nathan his drink.

"I have half a plan to help Margaret," I said in a hushed voice.

"What do you mean half of a plan? Just let the doctors handle it."

"Yeah, trusting mortals, that's not how I role."

He sighed and swiped his hand over his face, with his fingers lingering over his mouth. "Alright, what did you have in mind."

"I can perform a healing ritual. She will be well and ready to leave in no time."

"Then let's do it. What are we sitting here for? Go do your thing, help her," he said enthusiastically.

"It's not so simple. I need ginkgo, ginseng, milk thistle, and primrose for a healing tonic, like a conduit for the spell."

"OK. So, how do we get that stuff?"

"Well, I have a stash back home."

"How far away do you live?" His voice was rough with irritation.

I rolled my eyes and sipped my coffee. "It is about a forty-minute journey from here."

"Wait, we don't have a car," Nathan bellowed.

"I can call my friends to come back around."

"Or we can hail a cab."

"This isn't New York, buddy. How much do you think a forty-minute cab ride to my home and back would cost? Margaret is not in imminent danger. We have time to wait for Emma and Ryan."

"Fine. Just make the call," he said harshly.

"I don't like you either, just so we're clear."

"It didn't seem like that earlier."

"What can I say? It was a rare moment of weakness, Nathaniel."

"It's Nathan."

"Yeah, I don't care."

Nathan rolled his eyes in protest. I dialed the number and placed my phone to my ear.

"Ryan, how far away are you guys?"

"Not too far. We stopped to get ice cream at this cute little shop about ten minutes away from where we left you guys."

"I need you to come back and get us."

"What happened?"

"We got into an accident, it is kind of a long story, but I need to go back home and grab a few things. Can you guys take me?"

"Sure thing," Emma chimed in. "We cleared the entire day. Today is all about taking care of you."

"What would I do without you guys?"

"Drive yourself around." Ryan chuckled. "What hospital are you at?"

"Salem Medical Center."

"Ok, we will be there soon. Is anyone hurt?"

"Maggie is a little banged up. The rest of us have a few scratches and bruises, but nothing too serious." I glanced back at Nathan, who was staring me down intently, hanging on to every word.

"We will get there as fast as we can," Emma reassured.

"See you soon." I hung up the phone and placed it face down on the table.

"So, where did you two meet," I asked Nathan.

"I am not talking about this with you."

139

"I am just trying to be supportive. I know that earlier was an emotional lapse in judgment. I am attempting to make small talk and hopefully, we can get to know each other. Maggie will undoubtedly try to push me out of her life after my earlier behavior and I just wanted to make sure that she is taken care of."

He cleared his throat and sighed. "We met on 42$^{nd}$ street. She was barreling down the street looking down at her phone. She was trying to find the perfect mood music. Mags bumped into me, and I looked into her luminous chocolate brown eyes and found solace in her awkward, yet warm smile. So, I took her to the show I was in, and we danced across the stage afterward. When she was in my arms, the whole world disappeared. I felt at home."

I stifled a laugh. That is a meet-cute, a picturesque moment in fantasy. He was incessantly driveling about true love and love at first sight. That does not exist. Love only opens the door to heartbreak. That is how my story went. My parents' and countless others' love stories ended in despair and tragedy. Why did Margaret chase this? Why did she romanticize this? We lived in vastly different worlds. I prided myself on knowing the truth. It was a distraction from what really mattered, fulfilling vocations.

"What is so funny?" Nathan asked.

"Nothing." I smirked.

"You made your feelings about my relationship quite apparent so just say what you're thinking," he said, irritated.

"That is a fantasy. Let me guess, you wrote her a song after?"

Nathan stared at the ground and sunk back into his seat.

"You have to be kidding me. What rom-com did you steal all of that from." I descended into hysterical laughter. Nathan stood up to leave.

"Sorry, sorry. It is just that this is too perfect. I mean, you whipped out every trick in the book. How could she resist?" I teased.

"Ok, since you know everything about love and romance where is your Mr. Right. I sure don't envy the poor sap."

"Well, wouldn't you like to know?"

"Yeah, I would."

"Well, like you and Margaret I was once naïve and in love…Yeah, that didn't work out," I said in a menacing tone.

"What happened."

"We exchanged vows, and then we were burned to death, with our skin searing from our bones, whilst screaming in agony, and making promises to find each other in another life. You know the typical way these stories go."

"I am sorry that happened to you."

"You know, three other people know that story and everyone always says the same thing. People always make that same face. Like, I must be damaged goods, broken. Well, guess what, tragedy builds character. Charles is gone to me forever. I moved on. I let go."

"Then why were you at the site today?"

"I was saying goodbye. It took me centuries to accept that our tale reached its final chapter on those stakes."

"What does that mean?"

"Well, if you must know, I found his reincarnation earlier today. He is married with a child on the way. So, I don't think a continuation of the Joan and Charles love story fits into his book. Maybe his unfinished business was her and never me."

Nathan shifted uncomfortably. "I don't know what to say to that."

"You don't have to say a word. Just help me take care of Margaret, today, and then by her will, you may never see me again."

"You were hurting."

"I don't think she will see it that way, Nathaniel."

"I'll help her reach the light." He shot me a reassuring smile and I returned his sentiment.

He took a sip of his coffee and I followed. I traced my finger around the rim of the cup and stared off into space. I was angry about the accident and Charles and Thomas and Felicity and Margaret's self-indulgence. My anger and envy felt massive, explosive, and overwhelming. These emotions felt consuming. I needed a break from my tragedy, my life.

"Tell me about your life, outside of Margaret," I commanded.

He rolled his eyes, but then he looked at me with the kind of gaze that penetrates barriers. I don't know what he sees or how he feels about what he sees. But his gaze softens ever so slightly.

"Family and friendships that feel like family are the most important things in the world to me." His gaze never left as he spoke.

"I like to make the people I surround myself with happy. I just want to make her happy, because she deserves the world."

I saw Nathaniel's appeal. He was charming, selfless, compassionate, and funny. He was a picture-perfect suitor. He is everything that Margaret hoped for back in the late 1600s. It was like, he had been plucked out of her favorite romance novel. He was her dream guy. I mean, he is a little generic, but still moderately handsome. He is intelligent, quick-witted, and slightly tragic. He was her perfect match. I could see how he balanced her out and most importantly, he knew our secret and loved her despite it. My phone buzzed and I turned it over. I read the notification.

"I told the nurses to page me when Margaret returned to her room. She is there now," I said. We both rose from our seats, holding our drinks, and made our way to Maggie's room. As we neared her room, I see Nathan visibly pale, and his muscle stiffen.

"She is going to be alright," I reassured. I cleared my throat. "By the way, I told the staff that we are a couple."

"You did what," he exclaimed at me.

"That was the only way they would tell me your whereabouts." I sighed in frustration. "Just make it look convincing."

"Fine, but don't get any ideas. I *love* Margaret."

"Understood. You're way out of my league anyways."

He scuffed and I grabbed his hand, interlacing our fingers.

"Your hands are sweaty," I recoiled.

"This was your idea," he responded, enjoying my revolting.

"I could dry them with a flick of my wrist, dude."

"We're in public. Can you at least pretend to be normal?"

"No, I can't be what I am not." I stopped walking and Nathan followed. I turned his palm over in my hand and whispered, "Siccum."

He pulled his hand from mine and his eye grew wide. "Stop, that feels weird."

"Oh, man up," I affirmed.

"Why would you do that?"

"Because your hand was slimy. And relax, no one saw." I looked around. A young doctor, probably a resident stood at the end of the hall. Her nose was in his book. She seemed to be calm and not privy to my witchcraft.

"What if she saw you," whispered Nathan.

"Residents are sleep deprived uptight scientists. If she saw anything, she would surely blame exhaustion and sleep deprivation."

"Well, you just have an answer for everything."

"Sure do." I extended my hand toward his. "Now, can we go see my sister, or are you going to freak out again." He rolled his eyes, and we interlaced our fingers once again. We continued down the hall until we reached her room. Margaret was awake but seemed dazed and out of it. A physician was examining her chart. Nathan immediately scurried into the room, crouched down by her bed, and held her hand. I stood by her feet at the end of the bed and gave her body a once-over.

I turned to the doctor. "Did she sustain any internal bleeding or ruptures?"

"Hello, Ms. Baker. I am Dr. Powell. Your sister suffered a splenic laceration, left shoulder dislocation, and a concussion. My team and I need to take her into surgery to perform an arthroscopic splenectomy as well as reduce the dislocation and perform a Bankart repair to prevent recurrent shoulder dislocation. We can bring her to the operating room shortly, I just need your consent to proceed."

He handed me a consent form and I swiftly signed it. I handed it back to Dr. Powell. I looked back toward Margaret. She was silent, drifting in and out of consciousness. I was worried for her, unsure of her pain tolerance. I moved to her side opposite Nathan. He was staring into her eyes and staring at her intently, he seemed to be willing her well. I understood his behavior, although it was erratic. We had a way to save her, to heal the damage. We needed to allow the doctors to correct the damage and once they release her, I can accelerate the healing process.

After several minutes, a few more physicians entered the room. They were going to take her to the operating room. I kissed Maggie's cheek and smoothed her hair from her face.

"You will be well soon, little sister." I walked around to Nathan and placed a hand on his shoulder. "Let them help her."

He stayed fixated on Margaret. My phone buzzed from another text notification. Emma and Ryan were outside. The doctors began rolling her away and he let go of her hand. Her bed was gone, and Nathan and I were the only souls remaining in the room. He turned to me, teary-eyed.

"Are you serious, man? My job is not nursing your pride." I scuffed.

He whipped his eyes with the back of his hand and inhaled deeply.

"What did you expect, a hug? Put your big boy pants on and man up, Nathaniel."

"Shut up, Joan."

"Are you done mopping? Because I am ready to go save my sister. Are you ready to tag along or are you going to hold us up longer with your blubbering?"

He turned to face the door. "Good choice," I mocked.

We silently walked out of the hospital. I walked in front, and he followed or sulked behind me. Emma and Ryan pulled up in front of the hospital. I turned around to face Nathaniel. "This is them. Get in and try not to be annoying." I opened the door to the back seat and gestured for him to get in. He shook his head at me and then proceeded to follow my demand. I got in after him. We sat as far away as possible in the confined space.

"How's Margaret," Emma asked.

"She's in surgery," Nathan responded.

"She'll be fine, but I want to make a tonic to help her heal faster," I said.

"Well, then. Let's not keep Maggie waiting," said Ryan. Nathan slumped over, resting his head against the window. I pulled out my phone from my sweatshirt pocket and reread the email from Thomas, formerly Charles:

Hi,

   My name is Thomas. We spoke earlier in the restaurant. My wife gave you an impromptu photo shoot in the bathroom. I hope I am not bothering you. I know why your face is so familiar. You're the woman I see in my dreams. I get frequent visions of you and me. It is like another time; we are in ancient outfits at a stable. Seeing you today felt like I have been around you before. I promise I am not crazy. Do you have these too?

   Best regards,

Thomas Allen.

He wanted to see me. More importantly, he remembered me. I could be a part of his life. The thought of seeing what I could have had with him but will never attain felt like a thousand bee stings to the heart, a tsunami could have been washing over me. After staring blankly at my phone for a few minutes, I worked up the courage to respond. I typed out the following statement:

Hello,

   Believe it or not, Thomas, you seemed familiar to me too. I don't think that you are crazy, and I hope you return that sentiment after hearing my

144

*theory/explanation for all of this. I shared the same sense of déjà vu when we bumped into each other earlier. It seems like we were close once upon a time, maybe in another life. I am glad that you reached out. I think that I may have an idea about what all of this means. I don't think this is a coincidence. My theory may even explain the visions. I am hoping that we can meet again sometime and talk about this in person if you'll indulge me.*

*Sincerely,*


*Joan Baker.*


    I reread and rewrote the email multiple times before sending the version I sent. I didn't understand what I hoped to gain from it. Could I survive just being his friend? Could I morally accept being anything more? He was an expectant father and a husband. He seemed to be a good one too. He was happy and loving toward his family. Do I really want to be the person to shake that dynamic up? Felicity was beautiful, generous, kind, and had a strong personality. She was giving him a child, a family. Can I compete with that? Ultimately, I want Charles to be happy. He deserves it. Back in our time, he wanted a wife and a family and realistically, I did not have any desire to fulfill the second half of that dream. What could I offer other than unwanted pain and tragedy?

    Our relationship was in his hands, and I hated it. I hated uncertainty, and not having control over a situation. I have always been that way, an uptight control freak. When Charles and I first started spending time together, he was the desperate one and I held our future together in the palm of my hand, which was uncharacteristic for a woman during that time. The man was in charge in every aspect of society, the dominant protector and provider. If he had it his way when we first met, he probably would have proposed on the spot, and I would have been mortified at first. But, after getting to know that amazing human being, how could I say no? Now, he dangled the carrot over my nose, waiting to relinquish it when he benefits. I don't know what lies in store for us, but one thing rang true, I wanted to be there for him, however, he and his family would allow it.

# 15. The Healing Tonic

I remained fixated on my phone, anxiously waiting for Thomas's response. Maybe he wasn't by his phone or is spending time with his wife. Maybe he is concerned with a more pressing issue. You would think centuries of searching for someone would make you patient. But now that I found him, I just wanted to be in his presence again. How much does he remember? Does she remember our vows and the death that followed? Does he remember loving me? If so, what does that mean for his current relationship? My head began to pound with unanswered questions and centuries of desires.

The car stopped; Ryan pulled into my driveway this time. I quickly put my phone in my jacket pocket and began thinking of my sister, fragile, injured, in pain, and in need of something to alleviate it. Ryan was peering at me through the rear mirror. I gave him a sympathetic nod, showcasing my appreciation for his assistance. I opened the car door and walked toward my door. I pulled the keys from my sweatshirt pocket and placed them in the keyhole. I fiddled with it for a few seconds before the door opened, and I stepped inside. I turned to close the door and Nathaniel stood in my home, shutting the door.

"I don't remember inviting you in." I growled.

"You know what's funny, I don't remember asking," he said sarcastically. "So, where's the witchy stuff?"

"You mean the herbs."

"Whatever. Let's just get them and go."

"You read my mind."

"Then let's get on with it." I rolled my eyes and let him to my kitchen. I opened my pantry and revealed my collection of potions and herbs.

"This is awesome," Nathan blurted as he stared in astonishment. He reached for a bottle with a ruby red liquid inside.

"Don't touch that," I commanded. He immediately recoiled.

"What would it do to me," he asked me in a concerned tone.

146

"It will turn you into a toad," I said sarcastically.

"Why do you hate me so much?"

"I don't hate you. I hate what you represent."

"And what is that exactly?"

I looked away from him and started gathering the necessary ingredients for the tonic. I found a mortar and pestle and placed them in a shopping bag that I found on the bottle shelf. I placed the other ingredients in the bag as I found them.

I mumbled, "milk thistle," under my breath.

"What was that," he asked smugly. I began to frantically search for it pushing around the items on my organized shelves.

"What's the matter?"

"It isn't here." I sighed in frustration.

"What isn't there?"

"I am out of milk thistle."

"Well, where do we find more?"

"The supermarket."

"In a supermarket?"

"Yes, hidden in plain sight from feeble human minds."

Nathan shook his head and rolled his eyes. "Let's just go get some."

"Gladly. The market is like two blocks from here. We can just walk so that we don't have to waste time with parking." I pulled out my phone and texted Ryan and Emma the developments and plans for our current situation. I led him out of my house and onto the sidewalk.

"Do you think, she'll be out of surgery soon," Nathan asked.

"Probably, Nathaniel."

"How many times do I have to tell you, my name is Nathan."

"Can you stop whining and stay focused?"

"Fine. We don't have to speak to each other. I just want to be back before Margaret wakes."

"Look, we actually agree on something," I said sarcastically.

We walked in silence. We entered the supermarket and I led him to the aisle full of herbs. I scanned the contents briefly before finding the milk thistle. I cocked my head in Nathan's direction, to find him smelling herbs.

"What are you doing?"

"What is this? It reeks."

"You are such a child. I got what we need. Put it down and follow me." He obeyed my order. I grabbed his hand and led him to the cash register. The line was short. I was able to purchase the milk thistle within a few minutes, and we began making our way back to the car. I would have been more efficient if Emma and Ryan met us outside the market, but the idea escaped me.

"Do you really think you can help her?" Nathan asked.

"That's the plan."

"When is the last time you did this?"

"It has been a while since I have cast this particular spell, but I know I can do it. I have successfully done it countless times before."

"Sounds, like you're a bit rusty."

I grabbed the neckline of his shirt and pulled him toward me. He raised his hands in the air to signify his surrender. "You best not doubt me. Those who do never make that decision twice. And many have lost that fight."

"Sorry, I didn't mean to hit a nerve there." I released him from my grasp. "I am sure you have everything under control," he said sarcastically. Enraged by his insincerity, I lunged at him, tackling him to the concrete. I restrained him and stared him down.

"You're insane and very strong for such a tiny girl."

He struggled underneath me.

"Woman," I whispered, before rolling over and releasing him from my will. "Try me again and know that I don't need magic to subdue you." He nodded in submission, and I smiled with delight. He stood up with a quickness and extended his hand to me. Ignoring his chivalrous gesture, I got up on my own and dusted off my clothes. I brushed past him and took the lead in silence on our way to the car.

# 16. Ghosts of the Past

We got back to the hospital in a nick of time. Margaret had just got back from surgery. She was still asleep, reeling from the residual pain medication in her system. The four of us sat in her room and waited for her to awake. My earlier attempt to allure Nathaniel seemed like lunacy. I was mortified by my actions and would need to atone for them when Maggie came to. We said some horrible things to each other. How could our relationship recover? What was I thinking? That is the problem, I wasn't thinking. Could she ever forgive me?

Breaking the silence that encompassed the room and the tension between Nathaniel and me, I spoke, "Why did you stand up for me earlier, Nathaniel?"

"What," he asked, turning away from Margaret.

"You told Margaret to 'to take it easy on me.' I would like to know why."

"Well as you know, Margaret can be excitable and you were already hurting, she did not need to harp on your shortcomings."

"I understand the sentiment, however, I can fight my own battles. I don't need you to defend me to my sister."

"You know most people would say 'thank you' and move on."

"Well, unfortunately for you, I am not most people. It wasn't your place."

He raised his voice, "You made it my place when you came on to me."

"You guys need to take it outside for Margaret's sake," Emma chimed in.

"You right," Nathan agreed. "Can you try not to be a monster right now for your sister's sake?"

"Someone is forgetting that I can immobilize him with the flick of my wrist," I sneered.

A smile and a shocked expression formed on Ryan's face. "I feel like I missed so much drama. I don't know what happened between the two of you, but I ship it." Emma gave him a nudge, most likely out of embarrassment, and I rolled my eyes. Nathan ignored Ryan's statement. He stood over Margaret with her hand in his. He rubbed the back of her hand with his thumb and then pressed her hand to his lips.

"Dude, you know she isn't dying right. Like, you know she is OK, right," Ryan said comically.

"I am aware," Nathan said roughly with a tinge of annoyance.

"Just making sure because you are being so dramatic right now." The room filled with everyone's laughter, except Nathan. He continued to show his affection for Maggie. He smoothed back her hair and stared at her relaxed, sleeping features. We sat in silence, waiting for Maggie for what felt like an eternity. During this time, many doctors and a nurse examined Maggie and administer the standard postoperative care. I knew if her pain was controlled, she would be allowed to leave later today.

Margaret's eyes flew open, and she wildly scanned the room.

"Baby, It's OK. You're at a hospital. We were in an accident. I am so sorry. That car came out of nowhere and hit us. I am so sorry I put you through all of this."

"I'm thirsty," she said, weakly. Nathan poured her a cup of water from her tray left by the nurses and helped her drink. She took a long sip and then turned to me.

"Oh look, the snake is here too. This horrible day just gets worse and worse," she called out bitterly.

"Well, aren't you a ray of sunshine," Ryan blurted. Emma slapped his arm.

"You stick around this one…" Margaret weakly raised her arm toward me. "And she inevitably sours you."

"I think this is a family matter," Emma said as she rose from her seat and pulled a reluctant Ryan with her out of the room. I closed the door behind them.

"Nathaniel, stand to watch for any hospital staff attempting to enter her room," I said. He obeyed the order, begrudgingly leaving Maggie's side. I poured out my ingredients onto the side table and placed my mortar and pestle beside them.

"What are you doing," Margaret questioned.

"I am going to take away your pain."

"You have done enough," she said coldly.

"I am your sister; despite the horrors, I have done. And I am sorry, truly, for everything. I want to make it up to you. With time, I hope to mend our seam, but right now, I can fix this. I can heal the body, not the damage I did to

150

your heart. And that pains me because I love you more than life. OK, so can you just *shut up* and let me heal you."

Margaret relaxed back onto the pillow and remained silent. I began mixing the ingredients in the mortar while chanting, "Da sanitatem."

I carefully slid down her gown, exposing her injured body. She winced at my touch.

"I know. I am sorry. You will be well soon." Nathan turned to check on Margaret. His intense gaze pulled me from my concentration.

"I am doing my job, you do yours. It is not that hard, Nathaniel," I sneered. He returned to his tasks, and I scooped some of the tonics into my hand and gently applied it around the surgical bandage on her shoulder and stomach while chanting, "Corpus curare." I did the same technique on her forehead. I stared at her bruised and pain-riddled body and continued the chant until the tonic disappeared into her skin.

Margaret sighed in relief. "You definitely got some forgiveness points for this." She chuckled.

"OK, but just so you know, I no longer have any interest in that man. I never did. I was hurting and didn't handle myself accordingly. But I want you to be happy with whoever your heart desires."

"I desire Nathan."

"He was always yours." I kissed her cheek. I put away my mortar and pestle, before signaling to Nathaniel to join us.

"How are you feeling, Mags," Nathan asked.

"Better with you by my side," she responded. Nathan leaned over her, and Margaret pushed up on her elbows and met his lips. It was revolting. The man was a bad kisser, probably the worst I have had in my entire existence, and unlike Margaret, I had experiences to compare it too. I turned away, giving them a semblance of privacy. I could hear her gingerly giggle and I was relieved by her happiness. It brought a grin to my face. The door swung open, and the sound ceased. A doctor, the resident we had seen in the hallway earlier, walked in. She seemed to have a strengthened resolve with each step, a striking determination.

"You are witches," she said.

"Huh, what are you talking about?" I pretended to be confused, clueless.

"Don't be coy. I wasn't sure earlier, but I can sense the magic radiating in the room. That had to have been a complex spell."

I gave her a devilish grin. "You're a witch too."

"That spell, the strength of your magic, reminds me of a legend, a piece of history."

"We don't need a bedtime story. Carry on," I said and turned back to Margaret and Nathan. They both stared in shock.

"You're beyond powerful and seemingly very skillful," the resident said as she walked forward holding Margaret's chart in her hand. "She should be in a great deal of pain but is able to have a make-out session with knock-off Rege-Jean Page."

I turned back around. "Why are you still here?"

"I think that your Florence Jones."

"She died in 1886."

"She founded a resistance movement in the year 1864. She is the only witch to date that can perform healing spells."

"How do you know so much about *her*," I scorned. The young doctor slid off her white coat, allowing it to fall to the floor. She raised the sleeve of her scrub top, revealing a familiar image tattooed on her shoulder. It was the double-headed snake, my symbol of war for the movement. It had somehow resurfaced with a new leader. Did they have the same agenda as they did when I started it? Who started it? Millicent and I built that group from the ground up. Continuing it without us was a disgrace, a dishonor to her memory.

"Why do you have that," I questioned stoically.

"Because I am a part of it. We are in communities all over the United States."

"Who is doing this?"

"What do you mean," she questioned. Her brow furrowed.

"Who resurfaced *my* work," I screamed.

"Eric Thompson," she blurted, startled by my change of tone.

"What's the problem, Jo," Margaret asked.

I turned to face her. "Just a ghost from my past coming back to haunt me."

"It's nothing we can't handle together, right."

I sighed in frustration and annoyance. "I sure hope so." I turned back to the doctor. "Can you just discharge us now? So, I can go deal with this."

"Right away. It would be my honor," she responded.

"Yeah, yeah, I am you queen, and you worship me, just make it fast." I pulled out my phone and instinctively opened my email application.

"Why must you be so mean to people?" Nathan asked as he gawked at me.

"She was annoying, like you."

"Guys don't fight. You are the two most important people in my life," Margaret whined.

"I am aware and that is the reason I tolerate him." I met Nathan's gaze. "If it weren't for how much she loves you, you wouldn't have a ride back home."

"You know what. I think I am warming up to you," Nathan persisted.

"Not a chance, Nathaniel." He rolled his eyes and continued tending to Margaret. I glanced back down at my phone. Thomas and his wife were visiting family in New York and would not be back in Massachusetts for a few weeks. As luck would have it, I planned to stay with my sister and her dreadful boyfriend in the city. For the first time ever on this tragic day, I seemed to have the best of luck. I responded to the message, informing him of the convenience and he agreed to meet me in Central Park in two days to talk everything through. Three hundred and twenty-three years after the worst day of my life, to the exact day, I reconnected with my sister and lover. I was surrounded by fiercely loyal friends and the pesky Nathaniel. Despite his disturbance and obstruction in my life, for the first time in a long while, I felt complete and content. It is my favorite color on myself, sadly, it is hardly seen in the light of day. A new danger or dilemma was rearing its head from around the corner, so my newfound contentment would be short-lived, a temporary lapse, but it could be handled on another day. I allowed my worries to melt away, exposing the new layer of protection, sun-kissed by genuine happiness. I decided to permit myself the freedom to bask in the glory and ecstasy of today, because tomorrow I must toil on, preserving against the newest possible threat.

# 17. Have We Met Before?

We left the hospital yesterday. Emma and Ryan dropped us off and then returned to Massachusetts. I made the decision to stay with Margaret and Nathaniel in New York City for a little while. Margaret and I haven't talked much since the incident. We exchanged a few words back and forth. It is mostly small talk. Margaret has taken some vacation time from work after the accident. She spends most of her time with her lips locked on Nathaniel. Their love is intoxicatingly crass. I have just ignored Nathan for the past day. I find him to be a nuisance, a zit on the complexion of life. I need to get out of this house.

I am supposed to meet Thomas this afternoon in Central Park. Oddly, I am not anxious about it. I just want to see him and soak in his presence. This is the moment I have waited centuries for. I twirled my enchanted ring around my finger and stared down at it. It represents so much love and pain, but I was more than ready to reopen these wounds. I have had two days to mull over the fact that I found him. And he remembers me. His circumstance with Felicity certainly complicates matters. I could not bring myself to think of her or the child. I choose to be selfish. For centuries, my life has been about finding those I love and now that I have them, I will not give up without a fight. I want to occupy a space in his life. I am owed it. The universe needs a balance for all the misery I endured. It is only right. I rose from the couch, which has become my sleeping chamber, and stretched. I raised my arms above my head, interlaced my fingers, and yawned. I began to walk toward the doorway, attempting to leave the room. Margaret met me in the doorway and shook her head at me.

"When did you become so messy," she teased.

"When you stopped talking to me," I responded.

"What do you mean?"

"We used to be so close and now we barely exchange four words. I am so sorry about what happened." I turned my gaze to the floorboards and sighed. I met her eyes once again and said, "I plan to make it up to you every day for the rest of our existence if that is what it takes."

"I know Joan. We are OK. I know that you were hurting. Nathan and I forgive you."

She pulled me into her embrace, and gently rubbed my back.

"So, what is on your agenda for the day," Margaret asked.

"I have a meeting...with Charles, whose name is now Thomas. It's kind of complicated."

"Oh my gosh!" She jumped up and down excitedly.

"Don't Maggie. I am not sure what this reunion will hold for us."

"He clearly wants to rekindle the relationship." She walked over to the couch and began folding a sheet.

"Maggie, he is having visions about our time together in the 1690s."

Her mouth gawped, and she dropped the sheet.

"He remembers," she repeated and covered her open mouth with her hand. I nodded.

"How? What could this mean? Does he still love you? You guys can pick up right where you left off. Oh, are you guys going to get married," she rambled.

"I don't know, Maggie." I sighed and swiped my hand over my face in frustration. She grabbed my hands and stared into my eyes.

"Do not fret, Jo. Everything will work out. The universe is pulling you guys together for a reason. This reunion is meant to be."

I smiled back at her and said, "I hope so."

"We might have boyfriends at the same time," she squealed. I shook my head.

"You are intolerable, you know," I responded.

"And you love me for it." She blew me an air kiss and continued folding the sheet and fluffing the pillows. I headed into the kitchen and put water in the tea kettle. I decided to take a shower while the water boiled. I headed into Margaret and Nathan's room. Nathan was still asleep. I began raiding the closet. A lot of her clothes were super bright or floral, not my style at all.

"What are you doing?" Nathan asked. I turned around and faced him.

"Looking for something a little less Disney princess and a little more Chemical Romance," I said. He chuckled.

"What are you looking for," he asked.

"I don't know, maybe shorts or a dress. Margaret is smaller than me."

"You can borrow some of my stuff if you want."

Margaret danced into the room. "What are you looking for?"

"Something to wear," I said.

"Oh, I have the perfect outfit that will look gorgeous against your ginger hair."

"I don't want to dress too fancy, Maggie. Nothing too bright or bubbly. I don't want to scare him off."

"Come on. Impressions are everything," Maggie said.

"Maggie," I hissed.

"OK, I will keep it low-key."

"Who are you trying to impress," Nathan mocked.

"Charles," Margaret said in a sing-song voice. She turned back to her closet and began pushing aside hangers.

"So, you're reconnecting with the guy. That is good. I didn't think you had it in you," Nathan said.

"What is that supposed to mean," I asked.

"I just thought you would be too sacred to pursue him," I asked.

"I don't know, maybe making out with me, sabotaging your relationship with your sister and possibly your chances with him."

"My greatest lapse in judgment," I sneered. Margaret cleared her throat and turned around holding a black t-shirt dress.

"I was swimming in this dress. It will most likely fit you because you are taller than me."

"Thanks, Maggie."

She turned back around and pulled out a jean jacket.

"You have to wear this with it."

"Thanks, sis." I kissed her cheek and headed to the bathroom. I showered, washed my hair, and put on the clothing Margaret picked for me. I stared at my reflection in the mirror. I liked the outfit. I looked edgy and felt confident. The dress accentuated my long legs and my hair pops against the dark colors. I headed back into the kitchen, intending on turning off the kettle. I was surprised by not hearing the kettle whistle. I walked over to the stove and saw a mug with a tea bag and hot water inside. Margaret was taking care of me. Was she no longer angry with me? Are we passed the resentment?

I sipped on my tea for a moment and Margret entered the room.

"Oh, my goodness," she exclaimed. "You look gorgeous."

"You think so," I asked.

"Yes, now what are we doing about that hair," she questioned.

"I don't know. I was going to let it air dry."

"Nope. I got you. We should blow it out and then wand curl it."

"OK. Do you wear makeup," I asked?

"No, but I do have a few things that you can use." We walked into the bathroom together and she began brushing my hair and blow-drying it.

"Alright, I am thinking about an old Hollywood curls vibe."

"Go for it, just nothing too extravagant. I don't want to scare him off," I said. She laughed.

"It would be his lost," Margaret responded. She began wand curling my hair for several minutes. "What time are you meeting," she asked.

"Noon."

"OK, I am almost done with your hair," she said softly. I thought of Charles and the love we shared. I fell for him before I even conceptualized what love could be. I felt safe and secure by his side. I hated the idea of being a wife, but he made me want it all. I would have married him formally if we weren't executed. I was a lovesick child, and I didn't want it any other way. Our love was easy and all-consuming in one breath. I was at ease as the memories flooded in and pulled me into its warm embrace.

"Margaret, you seem content, blissfully in love. How long did it take you to trust Nathaniel?"

"Are you worried about telling Thomas the truth," she questioned.

"No. That was a dumb question. Forget it."

Margaret placed the hair wand on the counter, unplugged the cord, and ran her fingers through my hair for a few seconds. She swiftly moved from behind me and crouched down. She placed her hand on my knee and stared into my eyes.

"It is natural to be a little nervous, Jo. You are reintroducing yourself to the man you once loved."

I drew in a long breath and nodded. Although she was wrong. I am not nervous or apprehensive. I just want to talk to him, to feel his familiar touch and humor. I want to feel whole again.

"You two already know each other at your core and love each other deeply. He will feel it too. You have nothing to fear, Sister."

Margaret stood up and hugged me in my seated position. I turned to gauge my appearance in the mirror. Before I could fully turn around, Margaret forcefully pressed down on my shoulders, and I turned to face her.

"I am not finished yet," she exclaimed.

"Sorry. I'll sit still," I said in one breath.

She fished in a cabinet and pulled out a makeup bag. She applied a subtle pale pink blush and mascara and gelled down my eyebrows. Maggie finished the look off with lip balm and a bold red lip.

"Alright. Now you can look," she mused.

I stood up and stared at myself in the mirror stunned. The outfit and hair and makeup felt like me. Margaret captured the essence of me so well. Margaret rested her head on my shoulder and smiled at my reflection.

"You are a sight for sore eyes, Jo."

"Thanks to you," I gushed.

"No, you were always beautiful. I just helped you see it too," she responded. She twirled a strand of my hair in her hand. "It's not fair that you're a ginger. The color against your skin is gorgeous…I." She paused dramatically. "I am so jealous."

"Are you kidding me? Your deep brown skin and long curly hair are to die for Maggie."

She kissed my cheek and danced out of the room. I stood staring at my reflection. I thought of the photo Felicity took of me. I looked hollow, a void of the soul I use to be. I was never as bubbly as Margaret, but I wasn't an empty, unfeeling zombie. That is how the picture depicted me. The world around me blurred as my parasitic grief and longing for ghosts of my past ate me alive.

Margaret pulled me out of my contemplation. She danced back into the room with a simple pair of black sneakers. They perfectly complement my aesthetic. She handed the shoes to me, and I swiftly put them on.

"I hope you don't mind. These are Nathan's. I took one look at the outfit and thought that his shoes would be the perfect finishing touch."

"No, they are great. Thanks, Maggie."

"Can I borrow your car?"

"I don't drive."

"What do you mean, you don't drive."

"I never bothered to learn."

"You have lived in this world for three-hundred and twenty-two years and just never bothered to learn to drive?"

"I didn't even jump on the horse bandwagon back in our time, what makes you think that I would be open to the idea of operating a huge death machine."

I began laughing hysterically.

"It's not funny Joan." Margaret pouted. She crossed her arms across her chest and tilted her head. Aware of her growing annoyance, I ceased my laughing fit and cleared my throat.

I wrapped my arm around Maggie.

"Sorry, little sister. I guess I will just have to take the subway."

"Don't worry. I will call us a cab."

"Us?"

"Yeah, you are going to need some emotional support. The last time things didn't go well with Thomas, you kissed a perfect stranger."

I cringed at her statement. "You are never going to let me live that down."

"It is forever seared into my memory." We laughed and headed out of the room. We stood by the front door. Margaret called a cab and we waited for it in silence. I scrolled through emails and texted Emma and Ryan, informing them about what is going on. The thought of seeing Charles again felt surreal. I could live off of this ecstasy for a lifetime.

Nathaniel finally emerged from the bedroom and joined us.

"Finally, ready to be a productive member of society," I teased. Margaret nudged my arm.

"Be nice, Jo."

"I will let that slide because I know today is important to you," Nathan said.

Margaret got a notification on her phone. She drew Nathan toward her and wrapped her arms around his neck. He bent down to meet her, and their lips locked. They kissed for several moments, and I contemplated clawing my eyes out. Their blatant disregard for company, while they displayed affection, was gross.

I cleared my throat and said, "I think the cab might be waiting outside." They parted ways.

"What's wrong, Jo? Are you afraid of love?" Nathan mocked.

"First of all, don't call me Jo! And second of all, no, I do not wish to see my baby sister eating your face."

Margaret blushed and shot my wide eyes and a sheepish smile.

She ushered me outside and we found the vehicle waiting for us. I embarked on a journey to meet Thomas. I did not have anything prepared to say or propose for the future of our relationship. I only knew that I wanted him close. I wanted to hear him say that he wanted to be around me. That he remembered the time we share. I wanted to hear him choose to be in my life.

I wanted him to fight for me. I fought on my own for so long. He was what my long life missed. When we first met, I prolonged the progression of our relationship. My multiple deaths and the loss of my parents and Charles taught me a crucial lesson. Take every opportunity in stride, and hold onto the people you love for dear life because life is like a raging black ocean. It comes in waves and the island full of the ones I love could be submerged at any minute.

# 18. Sense Memory

I entered the park with Margaret by my side. She was tentative to release me. Our arms were linked as we made our way through the park. I saw the familiar silhouette of a man on a park bench. My heart skipped a beat and my pulse quickened. It was Thomas. I began to walk faster, pulling Margaret along with me. She tugged on my arm, and I stopped in my tracks. She combed through my hair with her fingers and adjusted the collar of my jean jacket. When her actions ceased, I resumed moving toward Thomas. Margaret followed my motion.

"Maggie, I think I need to do this part alone."

"Oh, OK." She released me from her grip. "I will be here, when you need me, Joan. Go get him." She shot me a sympathetic grin and I paced over to Thomas. He was skimming over a book and drinking a cup of what I assume is coffee. He was dressed casually, and his face looked pensive. He was deep in thought. What was going on inside of his head?

I walked around the park bench and came into his line of sight. I plastered on an awkward smile, attempting to hide my excitement. In his eyes, I was a stranger, and I did not want to display an inappropriate level of enthusiasm.

"Hi, Joan," Thomas said as he extended his hand toward me.

"Hi, Thomas." I took his hand in mine and gave it a firm shake. We simultaneously took a seat and erupted into awkward silence and obstinate tension. He stared down at his coffee and took a long sip.

I broke the silence, "So, should we address the elephant in the room?"

"I guess so," he said as he met my gaze. "So, I have had dreams of us in a stable…in like another time period in old-timey clothing. Sometimes we are riding or read under a tree. It is all just so bizarre."

"I have the same…dreams."

"It is so weird because they feel almost like memories. Like, I have been to that place before."

"Maybe we have. Do you believe in reincarnation?"

"Umm, I will believe in anything that makes me feel even a percentage less crazy than I do right now." He gave me a shy smirk and I returned the gesture to increase his comfortability, acknowledging how difficult this conversation must be for him. He is completely in the dark, functioning with fragments of a long, complicated story.

"My theory is that we knew each other in a past life."

"That's an interesting take. Why do you think we are being pulled together now?"

"Maybe we weren't finished in our time. Maybe we were taken from each other or died before we could do or say something."

His hand fidgeted on the spine of his book. I stared down at it for a moment. He was getting agitated. Is there a semblance of the Charles I knew inside of him? Does he remember more than he's letting on? I needed to change the topic for a moment and put him at ease.

"What are you reading," I questioned.

"Oh." He cleared his throat, "Hamlet." A wide grin stretched and escaped across my face. He is reading the book, I read when we met. "Are you a fan of classic literature too," he asked.

"The biggest," I responded. I felt a surge of hope rush through me. I was certain, now more than ever, that Charles returned to me.

"I suppose I should have known, considering that you are an author," Thomas said.

"I have probably read, Hamlet from cover to cover over a hundred times."

"That is absurd." He chuckled. "Why do you keep rereading it?"

"It reminds me of someone I used to know."

"Do you have visions of this other person too," he chuckled.

"Nope. Just you."

"What are yours's like?"

"Hmm. Let's see." I tucked my bottom lip under my top one and stared into the distance. I pondered for a moment, contemplating how far I was willing to take this query. Should I inform him that we were in love and engaged? Should he know about our executions? Doesn't he have a right to this information? It is his life, and he deserves all the facts. But do I want to

162

take away his happy illusion and put him through the agony of our past? Would it be inhumane to burden him with that anguish? Should I be the monster that rips away his contentment leaving a shattered sense of self and conflicted feelings about both women in his life.

"I remember you throwing mud at me and riding horseback and reading under a tree together."

"Do you remember the fire," he blurted. His eyes went glassy. My jaw dropped, my pupils dilated and every muscle in my body tightened suddenly.

"What did you say?"

"Never mind. You clearly don't share that one." He let out a thunderous laugh.

"No, elaborate on what you just said," I persisted wildly. He scooched about half an inch further away from me, taken aback by my hostility.

"I remember a fire-filled room, being in a lot of pain, and your face. We are alone in the room, and the fire has no apparent source. It is a recurring nightmare that I have had for as long as I can remember." I slummed back in my seat and crinkled my forehead attempting to push away the painful memory. I didn't want to relive that trauma. But it seems like the memories aren't exact. We were executed outside at stakes surrounded by murderous humans, and I wasn't in this body.

"And I hear a voice from rooms away say, 'Ashes to Ashes…'"

I interrupted his statement, "Dust to Dust."

"You remember it too. What could that mean?"

I shook my head in unsurety and exhaled breathlessly. "Well, I think that some higher power is drawing us together for some reason," he said.

"I guess we shouldn't let down the higher power."

I laughed. "No, I guess we shouldn't."

"Can we exchange numbers," he asked.

"Yep," I responded. We swapped phones and placed our names and numbers on each other's contact lists.

"So how is Felicity," I asked gawkily.

"Oh, she is great. She's working in time square right now."

"Does she know that you're here?"

"She knows that I came down to the park. She doesn't know that I am meeting you."

I sat up taller and my facial expression became stoic.

"I will not continue to meet you this way. You need to tell her. She is your wife, Thomas." I stood up to leave and he followed.

"I know. It is just that when I am sitting here, looking into your eyes, I feel like I am where I am supposed to be."

"Thomas, you guys are having a child. I can't be a home-wrecker. Coming here was a mistake." I turned away from him and he hurriedly grabbed my shoulder. I turned to face him shocked, and the clouds began to drizzle. At that moment, I remember how our first kiss felt on my lips and the muscle memory of how his touch made me feel back then. It reminded me of the time we danced in the rain, admitted our feelings for each other, and professed our love. This was perfect, as the climax of a beautiful dream. I closed my eyes and took in the moment.

"I can't do this to another woman, Thomas. I can't compromise my morals on this. Talk to Felicity, the mother of your child, the woman you married, and then come find me and we will figure this out together. Until then, we can't talk, or see each other, or even be friends." I looked down at my feet and swallowed back the surging emotion. I faced him once again. "Goodbye, for now, Thomas." I turned from him and gracefully walked toward Margaret who was studying me meditatively.

"How did it go," Margaret asked curiously.

"I don't know. The ball is in his court now." I continued walking out of the park and Margaret staggered behind me.

"What do you mean? What happened?"

"I gave him an ultimatum. If he wants to be in my life, he has to be honest with important people in his."

"That was honorable Jo."

"I know." I stopped in my tracks and ran my hands through my hair out of frustration. "I wanted to leap into his arms and tell him my heart remained his. But I couldn't do that to Felicity. I can't be that person, Maggie! Now, he has to choose what kind of man he wants to be." Margaret rubbed my shoulder and sighed.

"He loves you. He will do the right thing."

"That is what makes me nervous. The right thing would be to forget me." I hurriedly began heading out of the park and Margaret remained by my side.

"On to the next calamity." I chuckled.

"The resistance movement," Margaret questioned.

"Bingo."

"What are you going to do?"

"I am going to do what I do best, incite mayhem." I smirked. Margaret's eyes grew wide, but she did not ask me to elaborate. She stared at me blankly, refusing to allow her expression to reveal her thoughts. I grasped her hand as we headed to our parked cab. I needed to head home and get to the bottom of this. Who was this leader and what were his intentions? I disbanded this group and always intended to return to it once I found my loved ones. Now is the time and I am reclaiming what is mine. This man is no match. I have practiced for over three centuries. There is no widely known spell in our community that I haven't read and mastered. I am prepared to put up a hellish fight.

# 19. Motus

I slept soundly that night, still overjoyed by the splendid day spent with my semblance of home, my sister. I rose from my makeshift bed, the living room couch, with new vigor. There was work to be done. I rose and the rising sun peered through the window and graced the room. I slipped on some workout clothes, baggy shorts, and an oversized T-shirt, that Margaret laid out for me. I tied my hair up into a ponytail and put on my sneakers. I headed outside and jogged around the neighborhood for about thirty minutes, before heading back. I used the jog to clear my head and help me to focus on the task ahead. I did all I could do with Thomas. Now the ball is in his court. He needs to decide who he wants and the kind of man he wants to be. I found comfort in the cool breeze blowing against my body, the rush of adrenaline, the release of endorphins, and the secretion of dopamine. I recognized the beauty of the city. The semi-quiet that surrounds the city in the morning. It reminded me of myself. A city that was always moving, unable to sit still.

I entered the apartment and was greeted by Margaret as she tidied after me.

"Someone looks happy," Margaret said in a sing-song voice.

"Yes. I am ready to get to the bottom of our latest mystery," I responded. I approached the couch next to her and began helping her fold the sheet. "So, where is lover boy?"

"He went to a theatre workshop. He is teaching now," she said as she focused on the task.

"Oh, that's good."

"Yeah, he is really excited about it." She beamed as she placed the folded sheet back onto the couch and began fluffing the pillows. "So, do you want some help with resistance research," she asks shyly.

"Umm, sure," I said questioningly.

"Why the hesitation," she asked defensively.

"You have been vocal about how you stopped practicing and the denial of the supernatural side of yourself."

She crossed her arms defensively and sighed. "I see myself becoming consumed with my relationship with Nathan and I just ignored it because, after centuries of drowning in grief, I was finally happy. I need to find myself and define myself as an individual. I think that accepting my witch side is the first step in the right direction."

A smile stretched across my face. I gave her a bear hug and exclaimed, "I am so proud of you, little sister. We are going to have the best time figuring all of this out together."

I released Margaret and she danced out of the room. Her voice echoed from rooms away, "I am going to get my laptop and fix us some breakfast. You should shower because you are sweaty, and you smell."

I chuckled quietly to myself and rolled my eyes, I made my way into the bathroom and readied myself for the day, tending to my hygienic routine. Once I had freshened up and changed into a comfortable outfit for the day, I made my way back to the living room. The house smelled like our childhood hovel, the only place I ever felt at home. The familiar smell took me back to my happy place. I couldn't help but smile from the sense of memory. I headed into the kitchen and took a stance next to Margaret by the stove.

"Porridge," I said.

"Like mother use to make," she said happily.

"Look at us," I said pridefully. "We are talking about our parents and reliving our past without tears of sorrow," I said full of hope.

"I hope they are proud of the ladies we have become," Margaret said.

"I like to think that they are. We are together and happy and doing things we love. What's not to be proud of?" Margaret remained smiling and nodded to herself as she served the porridge. We ate at the island as she signed into her laptop.

"Did your movement have a name," she asked.

"Motus."

"Motus," she asked confused.

"It means uprising in Latin," I explained.

"Do we just google search 'motus'?"

"No, if they are smart, they probably hid it better than that. They must have some hidden code that allows only their inner circle access."

"A code? Like what?"

"Try Motus cauldron," I insisted. Margaret typed for a moment then shook her head, signaling my failure to encrypt the code.

"How about Motus's double-headed snake?" She typed for a moment again.

"Still nothing."

"Maybe, try sutom?"

"What?"

"It is 'motus' backward." She typed again and paused for a brief moment.

"I think we got something." She slid the laptop over allowing me to view the screen as well. I took a large bite of my porridge and chewed methodically as I glared at the computer screen. A website with the double-headed snake over a cauldron appeared. The site is encrypted. You need to solve a riddle to gain access to the hidden secrets.

Margaret read, "What is forged from the fire, but cracks under pressure and knows your every flaw and beauty?" Her face grew pensive. "OK, I am completely lost. What does that even mean?"

"It's a mirror. Heated sand creates mirrors, and they are reflective, examining your every flaw and beauty," I chimed in.

"You are a genius, Jo," Maggie said as she began typing in my answer.

"It was a lucky guess," I said meekly. The site accepted the answer and a second riddle emerged.

I read, "Retreat to the basics, and your access will be granted."

"What basics, like the alphabet or primary colors?"

"No," I chuckled. "Of course, the kindergarten teacher in you would think of that." She rolled her eyes and reread the prompt under her breath.

"I think they are looking for something a little more witchy, Margaret. Like basic spells."

"Oh, like a levitation spell or astral projection."

"That may work. Type it in," I said and watched carefully as she entered the steps to the spell. I was surprised that she still remembered it, considering that she hasn't practiced in centuries. I looked at her questioningly.

"Levitation was the last spell father taught me. I couldn't allow myself to forget it." I gave her shoulder a gentle squeeze and directed my attention back to the laptop. A phone number appeared on the screen.

"Should we call it," Margaret asked. I pondered for a brief moment. What could this phone call be about? Were there more security questions? How could I prove my loyalty to the cause?

"Call it," I said with a false sense of confidence behind my words. Margaret did as I commanded. I fiddled with my fingers in my lap as the phone rang. I motioned to her to be quiet. I needed to take charge now, and do the talking if they were to believe that I would be a complacent follower.

A man's voice said, "Hello."

"Hello," I said softly.

"How can I help you, Ma'am?"

"I am looking for Motus."

"Where did you hear about us?"

"My inner circle."

"What business do you have with Motus?"

"I want to feel a part of something. I want to learn about the culture that was ripped and denied from me. I want to reclaim my supernatural heritage."

"Are you based in New York?"

"Yes."

"Come to 100 Danbury Lane in Harlem, NY at 1:00 pm."

I heard a beep, concluding the call. I handed the phone back to Margaret.

"What did they say," Margaret asked. I slumped back against the couch, relieved.

"We're in. They want us to meet them at 1:00 pm today. Type this address into your phone. '100 Danbury Lane, Harlem NY.'" She did as I asked. I felt my phone vibrate and fished it out of my back pocket.

"Well, that is good right? We don't have to travel all the way to Salem to investigate," Maggie asked.

"Yes," I said not fully listening to her. I placed my attention on my phone's notification wall. Thomas was texting me. I read the message.

*Joan, I am sorry about yesterday. I thought what you said though, and I want to see you.*

My heart fluttered and my cheeks flushed. Did he take my words to heart? Was he willing to sacrifice his marriage, his livelihood for me? I responded to the message with Nathan and Margaret's address. I told him to come over and explained that Maggie would be here as well. He agreed to the spontaneous meeting and a soft smile formed on my lips.

I spoke softly, taken aback by the rush of excitement flooding over me. "Thomas is coming over to talk."

"Wait, he is ready to see you again," Margaret asked.

"Yeah, he apologized for yesterday and said that he thought things through."

"Oh, this could be the start of something special, Jo," she squealed. "I am beyond happy for you." She clasped her hands together and brought them to her chin as she smiled wide and judged my demeanor. "What are you going to say to him? What are you expecting?"

"I just want him to be honest about his feelings and then we'll go from there." I slummed into the couch and rubbed my temples lightly. "I don't know. This is all really complicated and messy."

Margaret scooted closer to me and grasped my hand. "Don't concern yourself with others' happiness. You have been doing that for the past three hundred and twenty-three years. You are allowed to be selfish, Sister."

"I can't in good conscious do this to another woman, Maggie," I said as my eyes filled with tears as I lust over something I may never have.

"You loved him first. You were his fiancée and recited vows to one another," she declared obnoxiously.

"And Thomas and Felicity declared their vows in a church, before God."

"God is everywhere. Your marriage, your love was real. You deserve this chance at happiness. I want you to have what I have with Nathan." She placed her head on my shoulder.

I whined, "Why can't we both be in love at the same time?"

"I know, how dreadful," she said sarcastically.

"Maggie, I don't know what I'll do if he denies me."

"Don't occupy your mind on those negative thoughts."

"But what if…"

She interrupted my statement, "And who's to say we only get one great, epic love in our life."

I nodded, taking her reassurance to heart. I needed to remain patient. This might not be all there is. How could I let this consume me? Distract me from enjoying the present and all the gifts it has to offer.

"Can you distract me?" Margret stood up and took my hand in her, helping me up. She led me to the living room. She sat on the couch, and I followed her lead.

"So, have you seen One Tree Hill?"

"What," I said as I pinched my face in confusion.

"I am distracting you with my favorite teen drama, duh," she said as she grabbed the remote from the coffee table and scrolled through her streaming service.

"OK. Show me your show," I said supportively.

* * *

We sat and watched three episodes before my phone went off again. Thomas asked to be let up. I communicated that to Margaret, and she disappeared into the apartment to do so. I think she stayed in the kitchen so that she was nearby for moral support. I was anxious to talk to Thomas but also appreciated leaving our label undeciphered. If I don't know what we are to each other, the answer can't hurt me.

About a minute later, I heard a knock at the door. I mindlessly headed toward the sound and let him in. He seemed shaken, worried about our impending conversation. I gave him a quick side hug before leading him to the living room and gestured for him to sit. We sat on the couch as far away from one another as possible.

"It's good to see you," I blurted. I sat tall, giving the illusion of confidence.

"Likewise," he said as he scanned the atmosphere. "Nice place you got here."

"It is actually my sisters. I am just visiting."

"Oh, I see." He looked down at his feet, avoiding our reason for meeting and creating an awkward tension that annoyed me.

"Thomas, why did you want to see me," I said bluntly. I could tell that he was shocked by my directness.

"Umm, I thought everything through. I know that we are being drawn together by some…force and I can't explain it. I feel something for you. When

171

we are together, it just feels right. But when I am with you, I feel like I am betraying my wife and when I am with her, I feel like I am ignoring a part of my heart that beats for you. And I am lost."

"Thomas…"

"But I *love* my wife. She is the love of my life. I am sure of it. You seem great and I think that maybe those other versions of us were happy but maybe they belong in the past."

These words stung. I felt like the twenty-two-year-old girl, tied to the stake, losing her lover, all over again. I had one last chance, one last-ditch effort to keep him in my life, no matter how selfish it may seem.

"You believe in magic," I said stoically.

"What?" His face grew pensive.

"I think you do and that is why you even agreed to meet with me. That is why my talk of past lives did not deter you. That is why you speak of it now."

"I don't know what you're talking about?"

"Please, don't lie to me," I snarled.

He drew in a ragged breath. "My great grandfather used to tell me tales of witches and warlocks before he died. The stories seemed vivid and authentic. I guess a part of me always believed in them."

I closed my eyes and extended my palms toward him, feeling his aurora. "I can sense the magic in you. Your power is weak from your lack of practice but it's still there."

"Are you magical? Was this past me like you?"

"Yes. I am a witch, and you were as well. And I think you still are."

"This doesn't change anything, I choose Felicity." I shrunk in my seat and turned away from him. The words cut like a knife.

He resumed speaking, "I am a married man. I recited a vow to my wife in front of our family and friends and God. You told me in certain terms to choose Felicity! So why are you so angry?"

Fury consumed me. "I am not angry, Thomas! Look, I know that this isn't your fault. And I don't want to blame you or hate you because you didn't remember me, or the time we shared but…I waited for you," I said as my voice broke. "For centuries." I slammed my fist down on the table. He shifted uncomfortably but remained giving me strong eye contact. "And I *hoped* and *prayed* that we would be reunited, and our affections would be intact but…" I chuckled softly to myself. "You moved on, left me in shambles, wasting my

172

love away while I try to find a man who already sold his heart to another." My volume increased. "And you have the nerve to ask me if I'm angry? I wish I could feel something so intense. I wish I could feel rage and desire to paint the city red!" I suddenly became more aware of my tone and my voice became more normal. "You left me numb and now you're a persistent dull pressure over my blackened hollow heart. I am not angry. I am grieving Charles, the man I used to know and I'm in a *great* deal of pain. I am in the deepest fiery pits of hell. And the man I love, the person who was supposed to love me more than anything put me here."

Thomas swiftly rose from his seated position and exclaimed, "I told Felicity about all of this. She was confused and worried and jealous. She accused me of being insane and hung up on my ex. I can't win here. Meeting you has destroyed my life. I just – I don't even know why I keep finding myself back beside you." He stuttered. "She...she left me." He sighed. "I can't seem to do anything right here. But this infatuation or whatever this is, is costing me my life. What do you want from me?"

I jumped up from my seat and yelled, "I want you to choose me! I choose you in every lifetime of my existence. Every damn time! Now we're together and I want you to want me too. My love for you remained consistent for centuries while your love waivers. That is a betrayal of the time we shared and the affections we held in our hearts for one another. I want to experience the love I felt at twenty-two in 1693. I want to read a novel under a tree in your arms and pretend that we are still there and all the awful things that occurred after that part were nothing but bad dreams. You made a vow to me. You were *my* husband. Does that mean nothing to you?" Tears began to stream down my face. I stared into his questioning eyes. I watched his demeanor soften. Was his love as strong as mine? Could he really understand the magnitude of our love without his memories intact?

Thomas looked me in the eyes and his expression hardened. "Charles made a vow to you, and he is dead."

I picked up a pillow off the couch and threw it at him. He stumbled as he dodged it.

He gave me a look of pity, an expression I despised. I am not, nor have I ever been, a weak, meager, defenseless figure. "And don't for a second think that I need this. I am not desperate! I just want what I deserve! What I fought for!"

He turned away and ran his fingers through his hair in frustration.

I chuckled to myself. "When we first met, I didn't want to be friends or even know you, let alone fall in love. You seduced me, you made me fall in love with you and then you left me alone for centuries whilst I searched for you, pushing away any semblance of permanence or romantic love in my life only for you to move on," I fumed, heartbroken.

Thomas made his way toward me, and I stood rigid. He placed his hands on my shoulder steadying me And I dropped my head refusing to look at him, the vessel for the soul of my lost love. "Joan, every part of me wants to love you in that way. But I just can't. I need you to understand that."

I picked up my head and looked at him numbly, "But what if you could remember. What if I could restore all that's been lost?"

He took a step away from me gaping at me. "I don't know…"

"Please, I can't lose you without you knowing what you're giving up. I have to try." My voice broke, "If you go through with the spell, I won't fight your decision if you choose Felicity." I drew in a long meditative breath. "I need closure with Charles, a proper chance to say goodbye without death hanging over us," I said fighting back tears. "Please just let me speak with him," I sobbed.

Margaret came running back into the room and held me in her arms. I fought against her comforting embrace and faced away from both of them. I took a long breath and wiped away my tears. How could I not be emotional? The love of my life, the man I sacrificed centuries for, my driving force in survival, dumped me for another. He needed to be clear on the magnitude of our love in the choice he was making. He needed more than fragments of memories to decide which woman he wanted to spend the rest of his life with. I understand that Felicity will forever be a fixture in his life, and I hate that I would be doing this to her, but Charles Roberts was the love of my life and I'm not ready to say goodbye. How cruel a fate? To know the love of your life is within arm's reach but his heart belongs to someone else. Fate seems to be playing a cruel joke on me. Am I not allowed love or happiness or contentment in this life or any other? Why can't I have this one thing?

"Fine. We can try," Thomas said sympathetically.

I turned back to them standing taller, my expression was stone. I was sure I could restore his memory. I just needed the right ingredients. The main one, of course, is the very symbol of our love, the makeshift engagement ring. I learned this spell in one of the grimoires I found in that abandoned house when I woke up in my second life. It was fairly simple. Elders used to perform it on patients with amnesia. All that was required was sage and an item that belonged to him before and after his altered mindset. There was no doubt to me that Charles would return to me today. If not in heart, then in mind.

# 20. Give Me a Reason

The tension in the room was thick, dreadfully awkward. I turned to Margaret. "Do you have sage," I said stonily.

She thought for a moment, her face was contemplative. "Actually, I do." She turned to leave the room when Thomas interrupted,

"Why do you just have sage lying around," Thomas asked.

"My boyfriend went through a crystals phase." She scuffed.

He faced me and his expression was perplexed. "Is she a witch too?" I rolled my eyes and chuckled brightly.

"Are you scared," I said sarcastically.

He stiffened, flexing his muscles. "No," he said unconvincingly.

"All of us here are supernatural. I trust you; I trust her, we are all safe," Margaret added amiably. He nodded nervously. I exchanged a tense glance with Margaret, and she swiftly exited the room. I kept my composure as Thomas anxiously paced about the room. I was determined to return what was lost to me.

Margaret returned to the room with a wooden bowl, a lighter, and sage. I stood up and retrieved the items from her and placed them on the table.

"You can take a seat, if you'd like," I said warmly to Thomas. He heeded my suggestion and sat down. I walked over to the corner of the room and crouched down to retrieve my bookbag. I reached into the side pocket and retrieved my makeshift engagement ring. I placed the bag back down and made my way toward Thomas.

"I am going to need your ring," I said. He hesitated, weary of my intent.

"It won't be damaged. I just need a physical representation of both lives," I said. I held up my ring, "This is a symbol of Charles and his vows to me." I folded my fingers concealing it. "Your ring is a symbol of Thomas. May I use it?" He handed the ring over to me without a follow-up statement. I could feel

176

that he trusted me. Charles was just beneath the surface, waiting for me to uncover him.

I lit the sage and placed the rings into the bowl. Thomas shifted uncomfortably. I ignored him and continued the spell.

I circled the burning sage around the rings as I chanted, "Praeterita meminesse tui." His eyes grew wide. My strange unfamiliar tongue frightened him. I found solace in the fact that the terror would soon be eradicated as his memory re-emerged.

"I need you to hold out your hands. I will place the rings in your hands. You shouldn't feel any physical pain." I felt guilty. I was dooming him to the traumatic memories that inflict on me. How could I let him relive the death of everyone he held dear? Terror took form on my face.

"I want to do this, Joan," he said softly. I closed my eyes and gathered my strength. I placed the rings into his large palm. I almost purred at his unflinching touch. I instructed him to close his eyes, relax and open his mind to what is being withheld. I took a few steps away from him and blew the smoke from the sage toward him. I watched as it danced, and swirled, drawn to the rings. From there, it moved up his arm, past his shoulder and neck, and entered through his ear. Thomas entered a relaxed, trance-like state. He slumped against the couch and his muscles relaxed. His lips parted ever so slightly as his past memories filtered their way in.

The rings hit the floor. I got down on my hand and knees, chasing after them. I found them both at opposing ends under the table. I grasped them and scrambled to my feet. I stared at them for a moment, symbols of two great loves. Who would be his last? I wish it was as simple as saying, "I found him first," but that is only half true. His heart belongs to both of us. Time and cruel twists of fate led us to this path. I believe in a higher power, a divine all knowing, all loving presence and I fear that he or she has a sense of humor. For I am a court jester, entertaining the lives of those who have mourned and moved on from me.

Margaret came and stood by my side. "No matter what he says, you will always have me." She smiled tenderly, placing a hand on my shoulder. I could not bring myself to look away from Thomas, but I could feel her unyielding gaze. She stared at me for a long moment before grabbing the bowl and sage and disappearing from the room. I walked over to the window and cracked it ajar. I needed air, a minute of reflection to process all that was happening. This is what I waited centuries for, this moment. What would I even say or do? Even with his memories, is his affection for Felicity greater than his affection ever was for me?

"Joan Baker," Thomas's voice called out. I turned around speedily. He hurried toward me, and I leaped into his arms. His warm embrace engulfed me and for just one moment I was that innocent girl in the stables. I could practically feel the wind on my face, the smell of spring flowers, and the warmth of the sun flooding through me. I remembered what it was like to feel constrained by society yet free in the arms of the person you hold most dear. I envied her. If she knew what was to come, she would have loved more deeply, danced through every grass plain, and sang the praises of every flower she saw. She would have saved her family. She would have lived one fulfilling, happy life and she would have been grateful for every moment. She would cherish every breath because before you know it, we all become dust.

I burn for my youth, for peace, for a feeling of completion. My heart is so heavy in my chest. It is a carcass caring for all the dead dreams for the life I planned for Joan and Charles. It's not fair.

I never did believe in fairytales, that things just work out for the best simply because you believe them to be true. But now, every part of me aches for a future with him. I want to believe in us, that things can be fair, that I can have a fairytale ending. I don't hope to be whisked away by a charming, dapper knight, although I wouldn't mind a pretty dress and waltzing the night away. I want to capture the euphoric feeling when you finish a good series. You close the last novel and a whole world of adventure, romance, and love flitter away and you are left feeling full. It is utterly euphoric. I want that more than anything.

"I remember. I remember all of it," he whispered. He kissed the top of my head, and I buried my face in his chest. Warm tears streamed down our faces.

I chuckled softly in disbelief, "I always knew you would return to me, Charles." I drew in a breath, savoring the moment. "Oh, how I have missed you," I said with a raspy voice.

"Please, tell me all about your life. I want to know everything. Don't leave out a single detail," I blurted out. I clung tighter to him, needing to bridge the gap between our bodies.

"Umm, I have two great parents and three siblings, a sister and two brothers. My dad is a retired lawyer, and my mother is an RN. My siblings are in college…I am the oldest child. We all went to private school our whole lives. I am twenty-eight years old. I spent most of my life with a book in my face. I played basketball in high school. And I have had visions of you for most of my life."

"Never let go," I whispered.

"I don't plan on it."

"You were truly the love of my life. I wish I could have altered the memories, remove all of the bad."

"I wouldn't change a thing. It got us here and brought you to me. I am so sorry for leaving you all alone."

I felt Charles take a breath and open his mouth to speak, "Joan, I love you, but…."

"Don't say anything yet. Just hold me a little while longer." He held me tighter. I could hear his rapid breathing, his quickened pulse, and the quiet sobs. Finally, we were together, and we would have to separate. Like Romeo and Juliet, we are lovers being pulled apart by the rest of the world. I always thought that story represented the stupidity of young love, but now it is a reminder to love with every bit of myself because it can vanish in a flash.

We remained entangled in each other's arms for what felt like an eternity, and I didn't mind it. For once, I was not conscious of time and impending danger. I just wanted to live in the moment and soak in every drop of happiness before my good fortune ran out.

He pulled away first. "The surety of my feelings only complicates matters more. I would have married you in 1693. I loved you. I think I still do, but I owe it to my family to try and work things out."

"You were the love of my life, Charles."

"And I won't be your last. I have to try with Felicity."

"But what do *you* want?"

"I want to never have died. I wish we could have lived out the rest of our natural lives together. I want to have married you back in our time. But in this life, I am tied to another. I must honor that union."

"I waited so long to be in your arms again."

"I know, but we must wait a little longer."

"I lived a long life. I have done everything I have ever desired. The only thing my world is missing is you. And I don't know if I can bear another minute knowing that you choose someone else."

"Don't talk like that."

"I can't bear it."

"Jo, I didn't know you. I was a new person with a dead man's memories, waiting to fulfill some unfulfilled destiny. I did not know to wait for you. I married my college sweetheart like the rest of my peers did. I was being painfully average."

"I don't want to exist in a world where we can't be together."

"Stop it," he grumbled.

"You can get a divorce. We can pick up where we left off, Charles,"

"I can't be the guy that abandons his family."

"Charles, I…" I hated how desperate his name sounded on my tongue.

"I married her." A silent plea died off in his throat. Grief hung in the air.

"We are eternally bonded. The universe has finally united us and you are foolishly fighting against it."

"Jo," he whispered desperately.

"Kiss me," I whispered. "Remember the way we felt. The feel of my lips against yours and the flutter in your heart when I neared. We can be happy together. If you abandon me now, I don't know who I'll become. I have been strong for a very long time. My heart can't take any more heartbreak."

"You can't guilt me into this. I need to think, to take time to process all of this. Let me go," he cried.

I released him. "I am serious," I said.

"You have the purest heart I know."

"You haven't known me for a very long time."

"You are Joan Baker. I know exactly who you are. And you're gold."

I turned from him and covered my mouth with my hand as I let out a soft sob. "Goodbye, my love."

"Dust to dust." He whispered these words and let himself out. This was our screwed-up way of saying goodbye indefinitely. My heart broke inside of my chest. I felt the hurt of losing him anew. The grief I had never truly processed was just buried under the hope of his return to me.

I stumbled into the bathroom past Margaret and locked the door behind me. I ran cool water and splashed it on my face. I felt sick, sick of not being loved, and nauseated that I let the lack of a man's attention bring me to my knees. I steadied myself on the countertop and stared at my dejected reflection, an all too familiar expression. I hated that it returned. I protected myself for centuries. I have been my sole provider. Charles or Thomas was not a necessity, yet I still crave his touch, his tender lips against mine, his warm, fragrant breath against the back of my neck.

I jumped up and down a few times and shook out my hair. I am and have always been a survivor. I am a witch. One of the most powerful of my time. This loss will not break me. Especially since he is not completely lost to me. At least, not to the extent to which we have been separated before. We were reunited for a reason. We had to be. This is not the end of the extravagant tales of Joan Baker and Charles Roberts. I will not allow it to be, not while both of our hearts yearn for each other to some capacity. I will love him with each dying breath.

I could feel a change in me brewing. My blood was boiling, scorching hot venom ran through my veins. A fire emerged in my gut and chest that had never plagued me before. Life was cruel to me. All of them.

I want compensation for my troubles. A way to make sense of all the hardship and burdens. I needed to find myself. And I don't care to play nice.

His rejection seems to bring out the worst in me, a deliciously wicked side to myself. Why be good in a world full of misery and cruelty? There is no use to it. The universe finds some way to grind you to dust. Dust, ashes, worm food, that was my story. Mine begins with dust while the average person's story concludes with it. Some would see my extended life as a gift. I think that I was damned, condemned for some long-forgotten mistake. I don't want to be a person people fear. But I am tired of hoping for better. I want it. I need it. In a fire, I was forged so fire I shall now become.

# Epilogue

Last on the tour of Motus was the gym. It seemed like a standard exercise facility. It wasn't anything special or exciting. Margaret, with Luke by her side, headed over to a group of relatively young, and fit women and men by the weights in the far corner of the room. I surveyed my surrounding for a few extra moments. I was looking for the metaphorical crack in their plans, a weakness I could use against them. I was drawn out of my scheming by someone's touch on the small of my back.

I cringed at the touch. "Fresh meat," a man's voice said sarcastically. I turned to face him with a callous expression plastered along my face. A tall, muscular brown-haired, green-eyed man stood before me with a boyish grin.

"Let's see what you got, newbie," he said smugly.

"And why must I prove myself to you," I questioned with my voice tinged with annoyance by his invasion of my personal space.

"Think of it as your initiation." He headed toward a cart in the far corner and returned with boxing gloves.

"You want to fight me," I said stunned.

"Yes." He handed me a pair of gloves and I took them from him.

"How do you know I can fight?"

"You look scrappy," he said sarcastically. He put his gloves on, and I followed.

"Do you challenge all your new recruits to a duel?"

"Only the ones who look like they have something to fight for."

I let out a low chuckle. "I could use an outlet to express my simmering rage."

He began bouncing. It was almost comical. "Hit me," he called out.

"I am not doing this," I chuckled. He threw a few fake shots at me. Aggravated by his baiting, I fell into his trap. I threw a few jabs and he blocked them. He countered and I dodged. We fell into a rhythm, like a well-

182

choreographed dance. I was anticipating his every move. Was he going easy on me? Did he mistake my femininity for a weakness? Did my lean frame throw him off the scent? I have been in plenty of fights, and I can hold my own. If he stood a chance against me, even on a bad day, he would need all his effort.

Beads of sweat formed on my forehead. This duel became tiresome. His breathing became more rapid. He threw a punch, merely grazing my shoulder as I dodged. I was getting tired and sloppy. A smirk formed on his face and a scowl on mine followed suit. Finally, I landed a punch to the gut, and he stumbled backward.

"You're a fiery one, aren't you," he said as he recollected himself.

I put my fist back up, squared to my face, and shot him a smile. "You have no idea."

He slowly approached me, and I clenched my fist. He gently lowered my raised hands and stared deeply into my eyes.

"What's your name," he said.

"Tell me yours first."

He laughed to himself. The sound made my pulse quicken. He was charming and our conversation was easy as if we were familiar.

"I'm Eric Thompson. I run this place."

My eyes grew wide, and I took a step closer to him. I was slightly shocked. I didn't expect him to be so young and childish. How could he have turned what I left into a thriving community? He had to have help. Maybe rich parents? Or older mentors? I wanted to rip him a new one for claiming my movement but instead, I decided to use my femininity and his advances to my advantage. I would make him trust me and then steal the rug right from under him.

I batted my eyelashes and gave him a soft smile, and whispered, "Can we talk somewhere, private."

His boyish smile returned, and he led me into an office, I suppose it is his. The walls are sky blue, and the furniture is white. It is modern and elegant. How can he afford to run this place? He can't be more than twenty-five years old. He closed the door behind him, and I dropped the love-sick fool performance.

He walked over to me and held my waist before I could protest and I pushed him off, appalled by his invasion of personal space.

"That's not why I asked you here! I am Florence Jones. You know, the infamous witch with thirteen lives that started this movement," I said sternly. "Does that name, and backstory ring any bells," I said sarcastically.

The boyish grin re-emerged and this time it made my blood boil. "What? Do you not believe me?"

"No, I believe you. I just didn't expect you to be so…"

"Fiery, I know you mentioned that I possess that quality."

"I was going to say young and beautiful," he said. I could feel the blood flushing my cheeks.

"Your flattery will get you nowhere. First, technically I am three-hundred and forty-five years old, so the young comment doesn't hold any weight. Secondly, I am way too old for you, so don't get any fresh ideas. Thirdly, I want what is mine," I growled.

"Well, you abandoned it. At least, that is what the legends say."

"And now I am ready to take it on again."

"Why did you leave it in the first place?"

"None of your business."

"Come on. You can't spare any details?"

"Don't be a petulant child!"

"Hey, I am twenty-five years old."

"I guess age is relative."

"You're avoiding my question. Why," he questioned.

"Because it doesn't concern you."

"Well, it is my group now. And if you want it back, you'll have to spill."

We started moving closer to one another, invading each other's space. I welcomed his pungent, aromatic scent. It was woodsy and herbal.

I crossed my arms and contorted my face in frustration. "Or, you can hand it over because deep down you know it is the right thing to do."

"And what if I don't want to hand it over?"

I was no longer interested in playing nice. He clearly wanted to do this the hard way. After the day I had, I am no longer enticed by a civil negotiation. "You really should have some sort of weapons check before you allow people to enter." I reached into my boot and pulled out a pocket knife. I placed it against his throat, and he held up his arms signaling surrender. His breathing was heavy. He was afraid but his goofy smile remained. "You stole from me.

You took what wasn't yours to take and I am going to give you three seconds to offer it back before I take something from you."

"It's not mine to give. Our community here choose me. If you want it back, you are going to need them on your side." He flicked the knife away. "And killing me is not the way to do that." I scuffed as I placed the knife back into my boot.

"And what exactly is your plan here?"

"I created a space where witches can be proud to be themselves. What more could I want?" His smile turned sinister.

"You and I both know that symbol that you have plastered everywhere means something else."

"You got me," he chuckled. "Man after over three hundred years your mind is still so sharp and cunning." I gave him a fake half-smile. "At some point, I hope to assemble an army of people who can fight if it comes to that."

"You want to expose magic?" I said shocked.

"Wasn't that your plan," he questioned.

"Yes, in a different political climate. You didn't even try to be original with anything. This is complete plagiarism."

"I don't see us fighting back for a few years now, but I think the timeline might be accelerated a bit now that we have you."

"I am no one's property."

"Wouldn't dream of it."

"You're the strongest known witch to date. You could help bring our people out of oppression."

"I work alone."

"That has to get lonely."

"You don't know me."

"Maybe I want to."

"Like I said before, flattery will get you nowhere." I tuned to leave. "Oh, and thanks for warming my seat. You're relieved of your duties, regent."

"Your inability to ask for help when you clearly need it will be your downfall, Florence."

I exited the office and made my way back to the gym. I searched wildly for my sister. A maternal fire burned within me. A protective, feral-like instinct to protect my baby sister and get her out of harm's way. I don't know Eric's intentions for me. He knows my true identity and he has the ability to make

185

my heart skip a beat. That makes him an unpredictable danger. I needed to find Maggie and flee, reconvene, and figure out how to win my people over.

I found Margaret sitting with three other young women. She was laughing and making conversation. I was rather impressed. Just a few days ago, we had talked about her unhealthy attachment to Nathan and now she is making efforts to change it.

"Excuse me. I need my sister back if you all don't mind." They nodded and Margaret stood up and moved away with me.

"We need to go," I said. I guided her through the new territory and toward the exit with a quickness. I need a moment to process all of this, gather the newfound information, and decide my next course of action.

Eric Thompson is such an unusual foe. I think I may have met my match. He's cunning, nimble, sarcastic, and quite the flirt. He seems to have a lot of heart. He might even be a halfway decent man. I almost feel bad for plotting against him. But he took what I built and there will be a reckoning.

"Did you find out anything useful," Margaret asked.

"I believe so," I said blankly.

"What did you do, Jo," she asked nervously.

"Oh, dear sister…" I stopped in my tracks and brushed a strand of hair away from her face. "I did what I do best."